Henry Churchill De Mille

John Delmer's Daughters

A cComedy in Three Acts

Henry Churchill De Mille

John Delmer's Daughters
A cComedy in Three Acts

ISBN/EAN: 9783744783064

Printed in Europe, USA, Canada, Australia, Japan

Cover: Foto ©Andreas Hilbeck / pixelio.de

More available books at **www.hansebooks.com**

JOHN DELMER'S DAUGHTERS.

A COMEDY IN THREE ACTS.

BY

HENRY C DE MILLE.

WRITTEN EXPRESSLY FOR

THE MADISON SQUARE THEATRE,
NEW YORK.

JOHN DELMER'S DAUGHTERS.

—◆—

DRAMATIS PERSONÆ.

MR. JOHN DELMER, . .	*A wealthy Banker.*
MARTHA DELMER, . . .	*His Wife.*
MARGARET, . . .	*The elder Daughter.*
ESTHER, . .	*The younger Daughter.*
RHODA MANLY, ...	*Their Friend.*
DR. FRED. VAN ARNEM, . .	*The Son-in-law.*
DR. LEONARD WEST, .	*The would-be Son-in-law.*
PALEY POMEROY, .	*Their Friend.*

ACT I.

Scene— . . . . THE STUDY. - - - "Advice."

ACT II.

Scene— . . THE CONSERVATORY. - "Treatment."

ACT III.

Scene— . . . . THE HOME. - - - "Cure."

JOHN DELMER'S DAUGHTERS.

ACT I.

SCENE—DR. VAN ARNEM'S *study.* *Cosy, comfortable room.* *Doors* R. 1 E., R. 3 E. *and* L. 2 E. *Large fireplace* R. 2 E. *Alcove and bow-window* C. *back.* *Small table and chair right of table* C. *Curtain rises on empty stage.* *Cold light of winter's afternoon shown outside.* *Snow falling.* *Fire burning.* *When curtain is full up, an old-fashioned clock strikes four.* *Enter* MAID L. 2 E. *followed by* WEST.

WEST. Dr. Van Arnem will be here soon, you say?

MAID. Very soon, I think, sir. What name, sir?

WEST. No matter. Simply say that the gentleman whom he did *not* expect has arrived. (MAID *gives astonished look, then exit* R. 1 E. WEST, *during this, takes off overcoat, gloves, etc., making himse'f at home.*) Fred wrote me that he had a surprise for me. But I'll give him a surprise. Dear old fellow! we endured a great many hardships together. But from the looks of things he is through with them. Perhaps it's his success he was going to surprise me with. Well! I'll surprise him with mine. (*Sees dressing-gown on back of chair* R. C. *and as thought strikes him he begins putting it on.*) Well! cousin Fred, as you are not here to receive me, I'll receive myself, as I used to do in old college days. Cigars! A whole box! Oh! Doctor, how the patients must have poured in! I remember when we had to stop at half a cigar and put aside the other half till next day. (*He has meanwhile brought a cigar close to his nose.* *With slight start he holds it farther off and regards it.*) But there were very few patients the day these were bought. (*He has thrown down the first one and picked up a second.* *Same bus.*) Very! He had to economize. (*Same bus. with box.*) It's my fixed opinion that he hadn't one patient. However, as I am going back to old times, why—(*lighting cigar.*) Ah! the odor is full of reminiscence. (*Crosses* C.) Let's see. Fred always sat nearest the fire. (*After a moment's hesitation.*) Yes, here was my place. (*Sits in arm-chair* L. C., *taking up book, which he opens.* *Enter,* R. U. E., PALEY POMEROY. *He stands for a moment amazed at sight of* WEST, *then crosses* C., *a little back of*

WEST.)   And our old protégé, Paley Pomeroy ; I suppose he must be here.   (*Thoughtfully.*)

PALEY.   He is.

WEST.   (*Starts and turns.*)   Paley Pomeroy !

PALEY.   L—Leonard West!   Is it really you?

WEST.   What ? not believe the testimony of your own eyes ? Then feel.   (*Extends his hand.*)

PALEY.   Oh ! be thou a spirit of health or goblin—

WEST.   (*Laughing and raising his hand reprovingly.*)   Oh !

PALEY.   Bring with thee airs from heaven, or blasts from—

WEST.   Oh !

PALEY.   I'll call thee—

WEST.   Father ?

PALEY.   No—nearer.   (*Extending hand.   They meet and shake hands.   PALEY looks wonderingly at dressing-gown, then at WEST.*)

WEST.   Yes, Fred's.   I want to astonish him.

PALEY.   You'll do it.

WEST.   Yes, I always did have my own way of doing things, didn't I ?

PALEY.   Yes, and from present appearances (*indicating dressing-gown*), you haven't changed a particle.

WEST.   It doesn't seem three years since I bade you and Fred good-by, to practise medicine out West.

PALEY.   The glorious West !

WEST.   Ah ! yes ; Colorado especially.   Charming climate ! So delightful, so healthy, that if I hadn't taken to mining and railroading, 1 should have starved.

PALEY.   Then you didn't have many patients?

WEST.   Not *many*—but *much.*   I was the most patient man in Colorado.   Waited three months before I had a call, and then the fellow died before I reached him.

PALEY.   Frightened to death, probably, at the thought of your inexperience.

WEST.   No, old age.   People out there suffer from only two complaints—old age and bullets.   Old age and sure bullets put a man out of the reach of medicine.   But, no matter about me. Tell me of Fred.   When I inquired the way to Dr. Van Arnem's, I was astounded at being directed to such a palatial residence.

PALEY.   Oh ! this isn't Fred's house.

WEST.   Whose, then ?

PALEY.   His father-in-law's.

WEST.   Fred married ?

PALEY.   The most married man you ever saw.   He's been counting on surprising you with it.

WEST.   Oh ! that's his surprise, eh ?   Whom did he marry ?

PALEY.   Miss Delmer, her papa and mamma—especially mamma.

WEST.   Miss Delmer?

PALEY.   The daughter of John Delmer.

WEST.   Whose daughter ?

PALEY.   John Delmer's.

WEST. The banker? (PALEY *nods.* WEST *hurriedly pulls off dressing-gown and resumes coat during the following.*) That settles it.

PALEY. Settles what?

WEST. Settles me. I'm going.

PALEY. What's the matter?

WEST. Three years ago I wrote to John Delmer's daughter that I would call upon her in the month of December, 1883. Evidently she thought it best not to wait.

PALEY. What did you intend?

WEST. To marry her.

PALEY. (*Staggering back.*) You—marry—Esther.

WEST. Esther? Who's Esther?

PALEY. Fred's wife.

WEST. Her name is Margaret.

PALEY. That's her sister.

WEST. Sister! (*Collapses, sinking in chair.*) Then John Delmer has *more* than *one* daughter—

PALEY. Certainly. He has two—Esther and Margaret.

WEST. (*After a pause, looking up at ceiling.*) *Both* married?

PALEY. Only Esther. Margaret is not.

WEST. (*Sigh, smile, and shakes his head at* PALEY.) Paley, you stupid!—I thought it a singular coincidence that Fred and the Delmers should both be living here at Tarrytown. Fortunate for me, though, for Fred could give me information of Margaret. I thought, you know, that *he* living near—but I never dreamed it was *so* near.

PALEY. (*Sighs.*) Yes (*meaningly*), *very* near.

WEST. And so Fred has married into the Delmer family. (*Jumping up.*) How in the world did it happen?

PALEY. Fred was the family physician. Esther was taken suddenly and dangerously ill. Of course Fred saved her life.

WEST. Getting their lives saved seems to run in the Delmer family. *I* saved Margaret's life three years ago; pulled her out from under a steamboat on the Mississippi; and, in pulling *her* out, *I* fell *in*—in love with her.

PALEY. Three years ago? Been waiting three years?

WEST. Oh! the old *reason.* Her parents, their pride, and my pocket, three very powerful p's, naturally brought us to a fourth—parting. (*Sings.*) "We parted by the river, she and I"—the Mississippi—down at New Orleans.

PALEY. I see.

WEST. Yes, but I'm puzzled.

PALEY. Why?

WEST. Fred was as poor as I was. Why should they take him for a son-in-law any more than me?

PALEY. Can't say; but they did; and, what's more, they took him right in—into the family. They fitted up these superb apartments for the young couple, and Fred has everything he wants.

WEST. Then all this is— (*Looking around.*)

PALEY. (*Meekly.*) Papa's; everything papa's. (*Observing cigar in* WEST'*s hand, he raises* WEST'*s hand to within a foot of his nose, holds it off again, then to* WEST.) Out of that box?

WEST. Yes.

PALEY. Papa's. (WEST *crosses to fireplace and throws cigar away.*)

WEST. I see. Poor Fred ; my poor cousin !

PALEY. *Poor* cousin ?

WEST. I said " poor cousin !" It's as clear as day to me. Mr. John Delmer was not in society. Here was a chance. Dr. Fred Van Arnem had position : all Delmer's money couldn't buy it for *him*, nor all Fred's poverty take it from *him*.

PALEY. But no blame to Fred ; Esther is the sweetest—

WEST. Don't say a word ; if she's anything like Margaret, I haven't a reproach for Fred.

PALEY. Still, I'm afraid he finds there's too much papa-in-law and mamma-in-law mixed in his matrimonial cup.

WEST. Very likely.

PALEY. Things are not as they should be.

WEST. They are not ! Then I consider it my sacred duty to help to make them so.

PALEY. What do you mean ?

WEST. Fred is too good-natured, undoubtedly—always was. I must help him out.

MARGARET. (*Without* R. 1 E.) Rhoda !

WEST. The voice of Margaret !

MARG. Rhoda !

WEST. Rhoda ! Another. I thought there were only two.

PALEY. Rhoda is a friend of theirs just from the South— (*enthusiastically clasping his hands*)—and she is simply—

WEST. Hello ! Hello ! (PALEY *checks himself.*) Is she rich ?

PALEY. No ; poor, but there's no harm in loving her.

WEST. Oh I go in and win. I haven't come back from the West as poor as I was, and I've a place for you, Paley, that will make you independent.

MARG. (*Outside.*) Where are you, Rhoda ?

PALEY. She's coming in here.

WEST. I can't meet Margaret y—yet. Get your hat and join me outside.

Exit PALEY R. 3 E. WEST *goes up to door* L. 2 E.

WEST. Ah ! you impulsive boys ! I'm glad I'm here to look after you—Margaret. (*Exit* L. 2 E.)

Enter R. 1 E. MARGARET. RHODA *appears at door* R. 1 E.

MARG. Come in, Rhoda. (RHODA *enters and approaches* MARGARET.) I'm going to order the sleigh. I love to drive when it's snowing. It's glorious.

RHODA. Well, I'll be ready. Here is Dr. West's letter. I've read it all through. (*Taking a letter tied with ribbon from her pocket and giving it to her.*) What an adventure you did have down there on the Mississippi !

MARG. You mean *in* the Mississippi, Rhoda.

RHODA. (*Laughing.*) Well, from what you have told me, the letter is worthy of the man. He's afraid of nothing.

MARG. Indeed he isn't. I told him we must never meet again, and he coolly wrote that he'd be here some time this month.

RHODA. Well, your first meeting had been under such peculiar circumstances.

MARG. Yes, under a steamboat. But this: (*Reads.*) "*I shall call upon you some time in December*, 1883." He would actually wait three years ! "*Should any one else meantime claim your hand, and you wish to bestow it—*" underlined— "*pray do not let* ME *stand in the way.*" Did you ever hear such impertinence ?

RHODA. (*Archly.*) I wonder you didn't instantly burn the letter.

MARG. (*Speaking carelessly, but tying the letter up with great care.*) I meant to, and I mean to still—

RHODA. You've been meaning to for the past three years, and you'll mean to for three years more. (*Taking* MARGARET'S *hands and looking into her face steadily.* MARGARET *with a half-deprecating laugh turns away and puts the letter in her pocket.*) Yes, dear. (*Watching* MARGARET'S *actions.*) It was very impertinent in him.

MARG. (*Thoughtfully, half to herself.*) Oh! if he didn't think that my father and mother were—vulgar ! Do you know, Rhoda, I sometimes fear they were wrong to give Esther and me an education better than their own. Dear little Esther !— no, she sees nothing different in them. Until I met *him, I* never saw so plainly. (*Forced gayety.*) However, I shall never set eyes on him again !

RHODA. December is not gone yet.

MARG. Oh! he's repented long ago of his—I suppose he'd call it love.

RHODA. What do you call it ?

MARG. A passing fancy.

RHODA. I don't believe it.

MARG. Then why hasn't he written me since ?

RHODA. He says in the letter you shall not hear from him, until he comes to claim you.

MARG. Would he treat the matter so lightly if I were not the daughter of people whom he—despises ? If he didn't in some measure look down upon me, as he does upon my parents, *could* he treat love so lightly ?

RHODA. Margaret, I've read the *letter*, and I believe in the *man*. There's some purpose in his eccentric behavior.

MARG. Well, I hope he'll not come.

RHODA. You *hope* so ?

MARG. Oh! I confess that my father and mother treated

him—cruelly; but, Rhoda, you don't know what passed between him and me afterward. He is *so* proud.

RHODA. (*Arm around her.*) I think I know a pride that equals his.

MARG. (*Thoughtfully.*) *He* said mine was greater. (*Leading her to a chair* R. C., *and bending over her.*)

RHODA. I wish I could help you. You and Esther have been so kind to me, ever since we first met at school.

MARG. That reminds me. Do you remember what we said when we were leaving our old school?

RHODA. The vows we made? Yes.

MARG. Of love.

RHODA. Of gratitude. (*Kissing both of* MARGARET'S *hands as she holds them.*)

MARG. We promised to stand by each other.

RHODA. Yes.

MARG. That means that you must *let* us stand by *you.* Your dear father's death has left you poor. You must make your home here with us. I'm sure that, if you were to become rich and we were to become poor—

RHODA. (*Nervously.*) No, Margaret, no—

MARG. Fortunes are lost every day.

RHODA. (*Anxiously.*) But *you* are all safe; nothing can happen to *you.*

MARG. Well, I hope not, Rhoda; but if anything were to happen, and you could help us—

RHODA. I would do anything you ask, to repay such love as yours.

MARG. Anything?

RHODA. Yes.

MARG. Then you must not go back to New Orleans; you must stay with us.

Enter MRS. DELMER, L. 2 E.

MRS. D. Why, Margie, I thought you'd gone to order the sleigh.

MARG. (*Crossing to door* R. 1. E.) Right away, mother.

MRS. D. Order the new one.

MARG. No, the other.

MRS. D. The new one is larger, and the neighbors haven't seen it yet.

MARG. The old one is cosier.

MRS. D. But there's nothing like our new sleigh in the whole neighborhood.

MARG. No, mother, I don't think there is.

MRS. D. I had it made myself, Rhoda. It cost seven hundred dollars, and still Margie doesn't like it.

MARG. It will attract so much attention.

MRS. D. That's what I got it for. I will not let people think we're poor. Wealth is nothing to be ashamed of. I want to let people see what we are.

MARG. But father is going to exchange the sleigh.

MRS. D. That's the way with everything I buy. Not two weeks ago I bought a lovely dress for Esther—three hundred and fifty dollars—and her husband wouldn't let her wear it, except in the house, and complained even then. Beautiful!— crimson and yellow.

MARG. If Esther wore it in the street, people would think—

MRS. D. We've money enough, not to care what people think.

MARG. *Never* enough for that. Don't you remember, mother, what the papers said?

MRS. D. About my dress at the Charity Ball a fortnight ago? But did it make us any poorer?

MARG. (*Arm around her mother's waist.*) Ah! but I don't want such things said about *my mother.* Now (*coaxing*), sha'n't we use the old sleigh?

MRS. D. Yes, yes—and instead of the black fox robes, put in common yellow blankets, and get your father to exchange the horses for mules. Will that suit you?

MARG. No, mother. Our own two handsome horses and the old sleigh. (*Going.*) I'll not be long, Rhoda. We'll have a glorious ride. (*Exit R. 1 E., laughing.*)

RHODA. (*Turning to MRS. DELMER, and speaking in low, hurried tones.*) Mrs. Delmer!

MRS. D. What's the matter, child?

RHODA. (*Hesitating and embarrassed.*) I—I must tell you something. I cannot keep it to myself—

MRS. D. Tell me, dear, certainly.

RHODA. Oh! how I have suffered since I came to this house!

MRS. D. You?

RHODA. Where I've found nothing but kindness.

MRS. D. My child!

RHODA. Margaret only just now begging me to make this my home always! If you knew the danger!

MRS. D. Danger!

RHODA. The great trouble that is likely to come to you all—through me.

MRS. D. (*Aghast.*) Rhoda! Wha—what do you mean?

RHODA. I—I'll tell you. You know about your husband's affairs in New Orleans?

MRS. D. Yes.

RHODA. He had a partner—Mr. Richard Varry.

MRS. D. Richard Varry! (*In alarm.*)

RHODA. You know what I am going to say. Yes, my father told me everything. In 1857 Mr. Varry left New Orleans for the North.

MRS. D. Well.

RHODA. As you know, the next vessel from New York brought the news of his death.

MRS. D. Yes.

RHODA. Afterward Mr. Delmer lost his own property by speculation ; but then, using Mr. Varry's, made enormous profits.

MRS. D. He—he did.

RHODA. But all these profits really belong to Mr. Varry's estate, and would go to his heirs, if they could be found.

MRS. D. There are none.

RHODA. If I could be sure of that !

MRS. D. Mr. Delmer searched and found—

RHODA. Not even a clue ?

MRS. D. No—Richard Varry was the last of the family.

RHODA. You believe so : listen. Mr. Varry, though a solitary man, was very fond of my father.

MRS. D. I remember.

RHODA. The night before he sailed he placed in my father's keeping certain valuable documents. Forgive my speaking of it, but what can I do ? My father was never satisfied with the search Mr. Delmer made for the heirs, and he intrusted to me a packet—

MRS. D. A packet ?

RHODA. Containing Mr. Varry's partnership papers, charging me, if it were ever possible, to give them to their rightful owners.

MRS. D. Wh—what ! No ! no ! impossible ! True, we lost everything. What we have now belongs, by rights, to other people. But where are these people ? It was twenty-five years ago.

RHODA. And yet that packet ! It may, at any moment, bring ruin to your home.

MRS. D. No, Rhoda, no.

RHODA. Were there not relatives living here in New York ?

MRS. D. There were people of that name, as there are now—but—

RHODA. I'm sure my father had some good reason for doing what he did.

MRS. D. Ah !

RHODA. Just before he died he called my attention to what he had written upon the cover of the packet.

MRS. D. Yes.

RHODA. It was this : " *To the heir or heirs of Richard Varry, formerly of New York, late of New Orleans ; died at sea in the bark Mercury, some time in October, 1857. If ever the opportunity occurs, my child, do not fail to deliver this, by all your love for me.*"

MRS. D. Could he have known any—?

RHODA. Again, just before the last, he drew me down to him and whispered, "Remember—Richard Varry—" then kissed me.

MRS. D. Strange !

RHODA. Ever since then I've been in constant dread.

MRS. D. Dread ?

RHODA. Lest I should meet somewhere—somehow, those to whom the packet is addressed—to whom Richard Varry's money would then belong.

MRS. D. (*In fear.*) That must never happen! My poor child, I wouldn't think about it any more. It's all passed and gone. It will never trouble you, nor my two that you love so much. You've said nothing to Margaret of—

RHODA. (*In a half-frightened tone of surprise.*) N—n—no!

MRS. D. If she thought her father had done anything which people could take exception to—you know how she worships him—she'd not spend another happy hour.

RHODA. She must *never* know.

MRS. D. There! cheer up. Your ride will do you good. Sh—sh, some one's coming.

Enter DR. FRED VAN ARNEM, R. 1 E.

MRS. D. Ah! Fred.

FRED. (*Opening door and calling outside.*) Yes, they are here. (*Listens.*) All right. (*To RHODA.*) Miss Manly, I'm sorry to drive you from my territory, but Margaret says you *must* get ready.

During this PALEY has entered R. 3 E., hat in hand, and is about to cross to L. 2 E., but at sight of FRED stops and looks wistfully at door L. 2 E., then at FRED.

MRS. D. She's coming, Fred. (*To RHODA.*) Take Esther with you.

RHODA. You'll not be angry, Dr. Van Arnem, at being robbed of Esther?

FRED. Oh, no.

PALEY. (*Aside.*) Oh, certainly not! Used to it.

RHODA. You're not jealous of my love for Esther?

PALEY. (*Aside.*) Her *love* for Esther. Oh, how I wish I were Esther!

FRED. My little Esther? Why, no; her heart is large enough for us all. She has my permission to go with you.

Exeunt MRS. DELMER and RHODA, R. 1 E.

PALEY. (*Aside.*) Much she'll wait for your permission after mamma's.

FRED. What do you say, Paley?

PALEY. (*Coming down C.*) I was remarking to myself upon the condition of the atmosphere—(*Aside.*) in-doors.

FRED. (*Sitting at table R. C.*) Yes, it's quite cold.

PALEY. (*Glancing at door by which WEST went out.*) It will be warmer after a while.

FRED. (*Takes cigar-box up, glances a moment at cigars, and pushes the box away from him, then turns to PALEY.*) Paley, old boy, toss me my cigar-case, will you? In the pocket of my dressing-gown. (*PALEY very nervously obeys. FRED takes up and begins opening letters on table. PALEY on other side of table, next the fire, strikes a match, but as he holds it for* FRED *to light his cigar, his hand shakes.*) Large mail this afternoon. Why, Paley, how your hand shakes!

PALEY. Large mail? Yes. (*Glancing at door, then with sly look at* FRED.) We've had the biggest *male* here this afternoon you've seen in a long time.

FRED. What the dickens is the matter with you, Paley?

PALEY. 'M bubbling! 'm bubbling all over with joy. (FRED *looks at him in surprise. He quietly returns the glance and points to letters.*) Over your prospects. Cords of letters there from college.

FRED. About my nomination. (*Having opened a letter.*)

PALEY. To the professorship. Ye—e—e—s.

FRED. What will West say? Dear old boy! Long time since I've heard from him. Ah! there'll soon be a surprise here.

PALEY. I think there will.

FRED. (*Handing a letter.*) Read that, Paley. (*Thoughtfully and half aside.*) I *think* I shall be elected; I've worked so hard. If this chance fails. (*Sighs, and strikes knee with hand.*) Oh! Paley, what is worse than a poor man?

PALEY. (*Without raising his eyes from the letter he is reading, answers quickly.*) Poor son-in-law! (FRED *looks up quickly at him, but he appears not to notice, and continues reading.*)

FRED. (*Having opened several letters.*) Ah! these are from some of my charity patients. (*Reads.*) "*Heartiest thanks for wonderful cure. Impossible to offer a fee to so rich a man.*" Of course. (*Another letter.*) Here, ditto—but with a sofa pillow. Where is it?

PALEY. Here. (PALEY *hands it. Their eyes meet, then drop upon the pillow.*)

FRED. This makes how many?

PALEY. Seventeen.

FRED. (*Sighing.*) If the worst comes, we can set up a shop, for sofa-cushions and slippers. (*Opening another letter, reads.*) "*Should be glad to have you for my family physician.*" Who is so civil? (*Turns page.*) "*The poor father of a family.*"

PALEY. (*Standing near alcove, throws the cushion down angrily.*) Oh, when Dr. West knows all this!

FRED. What's that about West?

PALEY. Oh, I was remarking to myself that we're going to have a storm from that quarter. (*Laughs.*)

FRED. What's the matter? (PALEY *continues laughing.* FRED *rises to go to him.*) Paley, what in the world are you laughing at? (PALEY *laughs all the more loudly. He is facing* L. 2. E., *and as he raises his head from a fit of laughter, enter* MR. DELMER L. 2 E., *so as to confront him.* PALEY *suddenly checks his mirth, and stares at* DELMER, *who watches him sternly. Pause.* FRED *resumes seat.*)

DELMER. You seem amused.

PALEY. I am.

DELMER. At what?

PALEY. At present, sir, I am not at liberty to state. 'Tis within my bosom locked, and I have lost the key. (*Looking slyly across at* FRED, *and pointedly.*) "Oh! Young Lochinvar is come out of the West," etc. (*Exit L. 2 E., singing.*)

DELMER. (*Crossing to fire.*) Fred, that fellow is a nuisance.

FRED. Why, Mr. Delmer, I couldn't do without Paley in the laboratory. He's a brother to me,—the son of an old friend of our family. When his parents died, my cousin and I took charge of him. He'd go through fire and water for either of us.

DELMER. Well, of course, if you feel that way about it, it's all right. (*Seats himself before the fire and rubs his hands, with the air of one using his own apartment.*) Quite a cold ride up from New York. You didn't go down to-day.

FRED. No.

DELMER. Should 'a' been in Wall Street. Northern Pacific four points at a jump. My work! (*Proudly.*) What d'ye say to that?

FRED. (*Carelessly, half abstractedly.*) Ah!

DELMER. Ah? Yes, to be sure; you're lucky enough not to have to make money.

FRED. (*Aside.*) Lucky!

DELMER. (*Taking out newspaper.*) Then my other little scheme! Ah-h-h! (*Self-satisfied air.*) Here's an article of mine upon it. (*Reads.*) "*Vancouver and Portland Railroad—best investment for small savings—sudden rise—great future.*" Perceive?

FRED. Vancouver and Portland? Where does the road run?

DELMER. Northern part of Oregon. But it is not built yet. (*Slyly chuckling to himself as he folds the paper.*)

FRED. The road doesn't exist?

DELMER. Only on my *books*—it's projected. It only cost me $40,000; but I've already got *that* back on the stock that's sold. I shall make double the sum. It's only a little branch road a few miles long. I doubt if it's ever put through.

FRED. Yet you lend your name—

DELMER. My name? Certainly not. *I'm* not known in the affair.

FRED. (*Crossing to chair L. C.*) And this you call business.

DELMER. (*Moving around to chair R. C., in which he seats himself.*) My dear Doctor, *you* shouldn't sneer at business. See here! Do you know why you are proposed for that vacant professorship at your University?

FRED. I suppose they think me competent for the position.

DELMER. Not a bit of it.

FRED. No?

DELMER. It's because you are my son-in-law.

FRED. Indeed!

DELMER. Indeed? Can there be a doubt of it?

FRED. I had hoped so.

DELMER. Then don't deceive yourself any longer. The Board of Trustees, with their blue blood, and their " first families of the city," may not receive *me*, but they can't reject my money. You are the son-in-law of Delmer, the banker ; he's worth money ; that's the family to select from.   Your *best* qualifications, my dear boy, lie in my cash-box.

FRED. (*Starting up.*) Mr. Delmer!

DELMER. You don't know New York as I do. Money, money, money, my boy, and money I've made in my *business*.   (*Pointedly.*) Don't sneer at business, Doctor.

FRED. (*Aside*)—The father of my Esther !

DELMER. Now I've made up my mind that you shall have the place. It will do honor to the family. And I'm not going to have you fail, because you're so blind as not to see it's money alone'll get you through. I place at your disposal $5,000 ; if that ain't enough, ten, fifteen. If money makes the mare go, by thunder ! we'll set the whole stable galloping. What's your personal income ?

FRED. About $2,000.

DELMER. See ? Why you can't even *live* on *that ?*   Did I ever grudge you a cent ?

FRED. No. (*Disturbed.*)

DELMER. Have I been generous or not ?

FRED. Mr. Delmer, I'll speak plainly. I *can't* stand this.

DELMER. Stand what ?

FRED. I feel like a trespasser on your bounty.

DELMER. Now cut that, Fred. Ain't you one of us ? Ain't you Esther's husband ?

FRED. Esther's husband !   (*Aside.*)—That's *all* I am.

DELMER. This money I allow you —

FRED. I shall not use.

DELMER. Then what do you build your hopes on ?

FRED. My pen—and my brain. If *they* fail, I'm not fit for the position ; if it can be bought, I wouldn't have it.

> *Enter* MRS. DELMER R. 1 E.   *She is about to speak to* FRED, *who has gone opposite* L. 2 E., *when* WEST *enters* L. 2 E. *and confronts him.*

What ! Leonard ! Leonard ! (*Rushes to him, catches both of his hands and shakes them heartily. Enter* PALEY L. 2 E.   *He goes down* L. DELMER *and* MRS. DELMER *have joined each other at fire, and watch the following scene in surprise.*) Dear old boy ! is it you at last ? I can't believe my eyes.

WEST. (*Arm over* FRED'S *shoulder.*) Paley had the same trouble. It seems there's a *general* want of confidence in the eyesight here.

FRED. (*To* PALEY.) You rascal. *This* is the surprise. I see.

PALEY. (*Aside.*) Wait till Dr. West opens on you.

FRED. What do you say ?

PALEY. Oh, I was only remarking to myself upon the un-
certainty of human calculations.

WEST. I don't wonder you mistrust *your* eyesight. (*To*
FRED.) We see more clearly in the West. (*Crossing, bows to*
MR. *and* MRS. DELMER.)

DELMER. Must have met you somewhere, no doubt, but just
at this moment—

WEST. I'll assist your memory. sir.

PALEY. (*Having watched* WEST'S *movements.*) The fun is
about to begin. Cool enough; but I think, on the whole, I
prefer the icy air of winter. (*Exit* L., *with look of fear at people
on stage.*)

WEST. One beautiful September morning, three years ago,
your daughter attempted to board the New Orleans steamer at
St. Louis. The gang-plank slipped ; she fell into the water,
and I—

MRS. D. (*Having meanwhile recognized him, draws herself up.*)
The sleigh will be waiting for us, Joseph.

DELMER. (*Repeating.*) Waiting for us. (*Slight bow, and
move as if to go.*)

WEST. You remember the trifle, I see.

MRS. D. I remember that you had the impudence afterward to ask for her hand.

DELMER. (*Always taking the cue from his wife.*) Her—
hand.

WEST. Which you refused me.

MRS. D. Very rightly.

DELMER. Yes, sir, very rightly.

WEST. Still, after *my* experience, I am rather surprised at
finding Dr. Van Arnem established here.

[MRS. D. and DELMER *show anger.*]

> *Enter* MARGARET R. 3 E. *She has cloak over her arm. At
> sight of* WEST *she stops in amazement and withdraws into
> alcove of window, unseen by all. She pulls one curtain
> partly around her, and listens breathlessly.*

WEST. Oh ! I say nothing against so excellent a selection
for your younger daughter. On the contrary, I think your
connection with Dr. Van Arnem reflects the greatest credit on
the Delmer family.

MRS. D. To hear such things in one's own house !

DELMER. Yes—own—house.

WEST. I thought I was calling on Dr. Van Arnem.

MRS. D. Then we'll leave Dr. Van Arnem to receive your
call.

DELMER. Your—call.

MRS. D. Your arm, John.

DELMER. Arm, my dear. (*He gives his arm, and they exeunt*
R. 1 E.)

> MARGARET *seems anxious to escape, but finding that im-
> possible, draws the curtain entirely about her. This*

action must be marked, as she is an unwilling listener to what follows.

FRED.   So it's you, after all, that saved Margaret's life?

WEST.   Yes. Her father majestically offered me $1000. I put out my hand for a certain greater treasure—the treasure I had saved to him—but he majestically declined to give it.

FRED.   You are very plain-spoken with them.

WEST.   It's the only way *they* can understand I'm independent. This parvenu cares for nothing but money.

MARGARET *is seen to sink upon the seat in alcove, still hidden by curtain.*

FRED.   I hope you'll succeed.

WEST.   Oh! they may still oppose me, but they shan't look down on me as they do on you.

FRED.   On me?

WEST.   (*Aside.*) Now to try him.—I could have told you, you were not the sort of man to marry for money.

FRED.   (*Angrily.*) You ought to know me better, Leonard.

WEST.   (*Aside.*) *He's* all right.—Then you love your wife.

FRED.   Of course I do.

WEST.   And she loves you?

FRED.   (*Tenderly.*) Yes.

WEST.   (*Aside.*) *She's* all right. (*Carelessly.*)—How long do you think it will last? (FRED *looks at him in amazement and anger.*) I've already had a talk with Paley, and I'm going straight at this business. Come, Fred, let's look the difficulty square in the face. Your wife's love, your honor, as a member of our family, depend upon—

FRED.   What?

WEST.   Your leaving this house. Your wife is a child now, but sooner or later she'll realize your position, when she *must* lose her *respect* for you, and then—her love.

FRED.   What shall I do?

WEST.   Break with these people, and make, for Esther, a home of your own.

FRED.   Home!

WEST. Free yourself at any cost. Our family are Knickerbockers, Fred. Let these—people see what that means.

FRED.   If it were not for Esther's mother—

WEST.   It is herself and her husband you must consider now.

(MARGARET *having come from behind the curtain and come gradually down* C. *utters a faint cry, and they turn.*)

Margaret !

(FRED, *looking first at* WEST *then at* MARGARET, *goes up and off* R. 3 E.)

MARG.   I have most unwillingly overheard.

WEST.   But you know that—I—

MARG. Cannot unsay what you've said.

WEST. Don't misunderstand me again.

MARG. You have left little chance of that.

WEST. You should not have heard.

MARG. It was most unfortunate, but it revealed that there had been no change in your feelings towards my parents.

WEST. Hear me.

MARG. It is plain, there is—there can be nothing in common between *us*.

WEST. Love?

MARG. No.

WEST. This is not the greeting I've looked forward to.

MARG. You know why we parted three years ago. You still look down upon my parents.

WEST. But not upon *you*, Margaret.

MARG. Speak of us together, Dr. West; they do not move in *your* circle, but they are my parents ; I am their child ; they may be unrefined, *but they are my father and mother.* In teaching Dr. Van Arnem *his* duty, your taught *me mine.*

WEST. Margaret, I do not blame you for defending your parents. I love you all the more for it. It is because of my love, that I do not deceive you, that I neither speak nor imply a falsehood, nor pretend a higher regard for your parents than I really have.

Enter FRED R. 3 E.

FRED. I've found Esther ; she'll be here immediately.

MARG. Gentlemen, I bid you good-morning. (*Exit* R. 1 E.)

FRED. Ah ! What's the matter ! Aren't things going well ?

WEST. No, they're not. And, old fellow, pardon me, if I must get some air before I see your little wife. (*Exit* L. 2 E. *abruptly.*)

FRED. Poor fellow. It *doesn't* run smooth.

ESTHER *appears at doorway* R. 3 E.

ESTHER. Come in ?

FRED. Yes, Esther.

ESTHER. (*Coming down.*) I thought Dr. West was here.

FRED. Yes, he was, but—

ESTHER. Didn't he want to see me?

FRED. Yes, pet, he's very anxious to see you.

ESTHER. (*Looking out of door* L. 2 E.). Takes a funny way of showing it, doesn't he?

FRED. He's disturbed about something Margaret said to him. It seems they are old lovers.

ESTHER. And had a quarrel already? It's always the way. Lovers without quarrels wouldn't be lovers I wish I had a necklace, with a pearl for every tear *our* quarrels cost *me.*

FRED. Would the necklace be a large one, Esther?

ESTHER. Oh ! very.

FRED. (*Sadly.*) I'm sorry.

ESTHER. How serious you are !

FRED.   Esther, listen to what I'm going to tell you.

ESTHER.   If you're not too long.   I must go to mamma immediately.

FRED.   Forever mamma !

ESTHER.   (*Shaking her head warningly.*)   See here, Fred. I've noticed, for a long time, that you have something against mamma.   You are unkind, and mind her wishes so unwillingly, any one can see it in your eyes.   I shall really be cross with you, dear, if you are not more attentive to her.   (*Suddenly and in quite a different tone.*)   And that reminds me.   We are to have a ball here in two weeks.   How do you like your little wife best ?   With curls or braids ?

FRED.   What sort of curls ?   (*Sleigh-bells heard in the distance.*)

ESTHER.   From the hairdresser's, of course.   What an absurd question !

FRED.   But you have such beautiful thick hair yourself.

ESTHER.   Now, tell me.

FRED.   Well, wear a simple white dress with a rose in your own hair.

ESTHER.   (*Drawing a long face.*)   Oh, dear !

FRED.   That's what you wore after we were married.

ESTHER.   At the seaside—yes; but here !—mamma would never consent.

FRED.   Why ask her ?

ESTHER.   What !

FRED.   (*Leading her to sofa.*)   Come sit down by me.   (*Sleigh-bells heard L. more distinct, as though sleigh were driving up to door.*)

ESTHER.   (*Running up to alcove and looking out.*)   There's the sleigh !   I *must* go !

FRED.   When *I* ask you to stay ?

ESTHER.   (*Seating herself beside him.*)   What is it, then ?

FRED.   (*Arm around her.*)   I wish this room were our house.

ESTHER.   Ah !   (*Wondering greatly.*)

FRED.   I don't mean literally.   But imagine a little house quite by itself—only for a husband and wife.

ESTHER.   (*Thoughtfully.*)   For husband and wife.

FRED.   Four pretty rooms.

ESTHER.   Let's see—parlor, anteroom, small reception-room, study—there are four already, and where should we eat and sleep and—live ?

FRED.   I can arrange them better than that.   A workroom for the husband, just out of the wife's room—

ESTHER.   Close by.   (*Assenting pleasantly.*)

FRED.   Not large, but very cosy.   You need only open the door, and they are together.

ESTHER.   That would do.

FRED.   A small parlor—

ESTHER.   Not *too* small, and furnished with Persian carpets.

FRED. If they can afford them. Then a pleasant sleeping-room, overlooking a garden, with the green elms close to the window.

ESTHER. Charming! Who told you about it?

FRED. What if I were painting from life? What if I had the cosy little house at my disposal?

ESTHER. You?

FRED. What if I said, "Come, Esther, let us move to our own home, where you will be mistress indeed." You'd go with me, pet, wouldn't you?

ESTHER. You are joking.

FRED. No, I'm in earnest. Will you go with your husband?

ESTHER. Away from mamma?

FRED. To our own home.

ESTHER. Haven't we everything here?

FRED. Too much, yet not enough. As a married woman you have lived in your father's house, just as you did when a young girl. Neither your rights nor duties are any larger. It ought not to be so. My means are not great, but I must provide you your own house, so that you may be the mistress of it.

ESTHER. And go wearing a kitchen apron and blazing cheeks!

FRED. When necessary. Good housewives are always ready for an emergency. As for me, I can no longer endure the life we lead here.

ESTHER. You are my husband here.

FRED. Esther, the man who wins a woman for his wife should take her to himself and be able to say, "She is mine —all mine—wholly mine." Rich or poor, high or low, it makes no difference. Darling, I can take you to my home, the poor home of a young physician. It is small and simple, but it can make us very happy. Do you hesitate?

ESTHER. Mamma and papa!

FRED. They have given you to me. I have undertaken to care for your happiness.

ESTHER. But, Fred—

FRED. Listen to me, little wife; you don't know what is at stake.

Enter MRS. DELMER R. 1 E., *dressed for riding.*

MRS. D. (*As she crosses to window.*) Well, dear, are you ready?

FRED. I want Esther to stay in with me this afternoon.

MRS. D. Indeed!

FRED. To meet my cousin.

MRS. D. What!

FRED. He is the only relative I have in the world, Mrs. Delmer.

MRS. D. I'm sorry, Fred, but (*looking fixedly at* ESTHER) Esther is coming with *us.*

FRED. (*Aside to her, tenderly.*) You will not go?

ESTHER. You—heard—mamma.

FRED. But *I* ask you to stay.

ESTHER. She will be angry.

FRED. Remember what I've said. This shall decide. (*Enter* WEST L. 2 E., *followed by* PALEY.) Ah! Leonard, let me present you to my wife.

WEST. (*Crossing and taking her hand.*) Delighted to meet you—my cousin.

MRS. D. (*Having moved to door* L.) Come, Esther, the others will join us at the sleigh. (*Exit* L. 2 E.)

> ESTHER *is going, when* FRED *lays his hand upon her arm and looks at her reproachfully.*

ESTHER. You'll worry me to death. Please don't say another word.

FRED. (*Thrusting her from him.*) Go, then—go!

ESTHER. (*Pouting.*) You're perfectly horrid. This is too much! '(*Crosses* L. 2 E.)

> *Enter* RHODA R. 1 E., *dressed for riding.* PALEY *having crossed* R., *meets her and assists her with her cloak.*

PALEY. There's a beautiful rosebud in the conservatory. Mrs. Delmer has given it to me. Will you wear it, if I get it for you?

RHODA. With pleasure.

PALEY. I'll bring it. (*Goes up and out* R. 3 E.)

> WEST *has moved to* R. C., *which brings them face to face.* FRED *has come down* C.

FRED. Ah! Miss Manley—my cousin, Dr. West. (*They bow.*)

RHODA. Your cousin? (*Crosses to* C.)

WEST. Yes, own cousin—indeed we bear the same family name—Varry.

RHODA. (*Starts and looks alternately at* WEST *and* FRED.)

> *Enter* MARGARET R. 1 E., *also dressed for riding.* As *she enters,* RHODA *moves back, with her eyes fixed upon the two men, until she meets* ESTHER *up* L. C.

RHODA. (*Aside in a whisper.*) Varry!

WEST. Margaret!

> MARGARET *coming face to face with* WEST, *stops a second, looks him in the eye steadily, then drawing herself up crosses him to* C. WEST, *as she crosses, speaks again.*

WEST. Tell me. Have you given your heart to another?

MARG. And if I have—

WEST. If you have, then I shall, in honor, withdraw. If not—

MARG. Well?

WEST. Well, I shall wait—
MARG. For what?
WEST. Till you are reasonable. Till you get to liking me.
MARG. It will be a long waiting.
WEST. How long?
MARG. Forever.
WEST. That *is* long—too long.
MARG. Nothing shall change me.
WEST. You are mistaken. *I* shall find the means.

MARGARET crossing to L. C., *meets* RHODA *and exchanges a word.* ESTHER *joins her husband in the alcove as if to bid him good-by.* MARGARET *crosses on to* L. 2 E., *and* RHODA *comes down to* WEST R. C.

FRED. Once more I ask you not to go.
ESTHER. Fred, I—no! not mind mamma? It's madness. Good-by, pet.
MRS. D. (*Without.*) Esther!
ESTHER. (*After a quick look at* FRED.) I'm coming.

(*Exit* L. 2 E.)

FRED. (*Looking half angrily, half sadly in the direction she went out.*) And I'm going.

Enter PALEY R. 3 E., *rosebud in his hand. He crosses and stands by door* L. 2 E., *waiting for* RHODA.

RHODA. Dr. West, the—Varry—in your name and your cousin's excites my curiosity.
WEST. You have met some Varrys, perhaps.
RHODA. I am greatly interested in some people of that name.
WEST. They are no kin to *us.* Fred and I are the last of our family.
RHODA. You have no relatives of that name?
WEST. None. We *had* an *uncle.*
RHODA. Yes—
WEST. Poor fellow! he died at sea in October, '57.
RHODA. And his name—
WEST. Richard Varry.
RHODA. Richard Varry your uncle?
MARG. Rhoda!
RHODA. (*Startled by the sound of her voice*). Yes, Margaret. (*With a frightened look at* WEST, *from whom she does not take her eyes, she moves to meet* MARGARET. *When* MARGARET *has taken her outstretched hand, with a quick clutch at her hand with both her own, her gaze still fixed upon* WEST, *she speaks in a fainter tone.*) I'm ready; let's go.

While this action has been going on, WEST, *having moved around the table to the fireplace, now leans against the mantelpiece with folded arms and looks at* MARGARET,

who, after a single half-defiant look at him, is urged off
by RHODA. WEST *with serious face watches Margaret,*
and RHODA *watches him in fear.* FRED *in the alcove*
watches the sleigh, with his foot on the seat, elbow on
knee, chin resting on hand. PALEY, *who has offered the*
rosebud to RHODA, *has been passed by unheeded. He, still*
holding out the flower mechanically, looks after RHODA.
at a loss to understand, and hurt at her apparent dis-
regard.

CURTAIN.

ACT II.

SCENE.—*Conservatory, back and right being of glass curving up*
from 4 G. *to front border. Doors* L. 1 E. *and* L. 3 E. *leading*
to house. Glass door R. 2 E. *leading out of doors. The in-*
terior is fitted up with plants, flowers, and rustic furniture,
the girders supporting a great number of hanging baskets. The
interior must be so arranged as not to hide the exterior, which
represents a snow landscape on a clear, cold night. Moon shin-
ing, crust on the snow, and every tree standing out sharp and
clear against the sky. A wing of the house, windows lighted, is
seen L. U. E. *Ivy on the walls and snow on the ivy. Footlights*
are to be well down; the light to come from above, as from moon.
Light also seen through doors L. *Dance music proceeds from*
house at curtain rise, and wherever available through the act.
Enter PALEY L. 3 E. *He glances around hastily, then crosses*
to door R. 2 E. *which he is about to unlock, when* RHODA
enters L. 1 E., *looking back as if expecting some one. See-*
ing PALEY, *she starts and sinks in chair* L. C.

RHODA.   Paley !
PALEY.   (*Crossing and standing beside her.*)   Yes.
RHODA.   (*Looking up at him after a moment's pause.*)   Well ?
PALEY.   Well ? Yes, thank you ; quite so.
RHODA.   (*Impatiently.*)   What do you want ?
PALEY.   I thought you called me.
RHODA.   I spoke your name—
PALEY.   People generally do, when they call me.
RHODA.   Because I was startled at finding you here.
PALEY.   So was I at finding you ; but I'm glad you came.
RHODA.   Why ?
PALEY.   Because I want to speak to you.
RHODA.   About what ?
PALEY.   Yourself.
RHODA.   Myself ?

PALEY. Ever since Fred and Dr. West departed angrily from this lordly mansion, a week ago, you've acted strangely.

RHODA. (*Trying to appear unconcerned.*) I?

PALEY. A weight seems to have been lifted off your heart. (RHODA *starts, and looks at him in amazement.*) When you returned from that sleigh-ride and found both Dr. West and Dr. Van Arnem gone, you suddenly became as happy and light-hearted as a bird.

RHODA. (*Rising in astonishment, and, for the instant, forgetting herself*) Paley, that is not true.

PALEY. I know it.

RHODA. Then why do you say it?

PALEY. To let you contradict. You're a woman. Couldn't make you confess any other way. There *is* something troubling you.

RHODA. Did I say—

PALEY. Now, Miss Rhoda, don't begin in the usual female way. I've heard you say that you've only two friends in the world.

RHODA. Yes.

PALEY. Couldn't you increase the number? Make it three.

RHODA. You are already my friend, I trust.

PALEY. No, I'm not your friend you trust, that's the trouble. Miss Rhoda, since you've been here you've treated me like a gentleman—I mean like a lady—well, you know what I'm trying to say. You don't treat me as most people do, and I feel— (RHODA *glances up at him.*) No matter how I feel. You're in trouble; *I* want to help you, and I'm going to do it. Will you trust me?

RHODA. Why, Paley, I—

PALEY. Will you trust me?—yes or no? (RHODA *looks up at him. He extends his hand. She takes it warmly.*) That's right. I had to hurry you, because we shall soon be interrupted. (*Moves to door* R.)

RHODA. (*Looking toward door* L. 1 E.) Yes, Esther's coming. She told me that I might meet her in the conservatory, to hear about the letter you were to bring from her husband.

PALEY. (*Unlocking door* R. 2 E.) And I expect a sleigh secretly at the park gate.

RHODA. (*Crossing and speaking anxiously.*) Who's coming?

PALEY. Miss Rhoda, I have noticed several stages of anxiety in you. When Dr. West suddenly appeared here a week ago and took Fred away, you reached the first stage; you were merely anxious. Learning from me that I was packing Fred's effects for a permanent departure from this home of ease and comfort, you became more anxious—second stage! To-night, though there's a ball in full blast, you don't show yourself at all in the parlor, but hurry to meet Esther, the moment you heard I was to bring a letter from her absent lord and mas—no, not master yet.

RHODA. (*Very eagerly.*) The letter! well?

PALEY. Third and last stage—most anxious! I'm stupid, I admit, but I *can* see that two and two make four. The young ladies are troubled, and you are troubled too—that's *one* " two"; your trouble has something to do with Fred and Dr. West, *my* two; and these two " twos," as the sailors say, bring me "to the fore" (*four*).—What is on your mind?

RHODA. What's Dr. Van Arnem been doing?

PALEY. Preparing a little home for himself and his little wife. He's taken a house just below here at Irvington, and were his wife with him, would be as happy as a king. At present, his frame of mind is not royal.

RHODA. Dr. West has made him do all this?

PALEY. Not entirely, but he advised it strongly.

RHODA. To take Esther away from her parents!

PALEY. Um-m-m! well—

RHODA. Then he is very bitter against them.

PALEY. Well, I don't think he adores them.

RHODA. He would do them harm, if it came into his power. Paley, I *will* trust you.

PALEY. Good!

RHODA. You want to aid me. You shall.

PALEY. How?

RHODA. This family's in danger of being ruined.

PALEY. Ruined?

RHODA. Dr. Van Arnem leaving Esther in this way, and Dr. West angry with Margaret!

PALEY. Angry with her? Not at all.

RHODA. Then why should he do as he's done?

PALEY. How?

RHODA. Since he's been in New York, he's done everything he can to injure Mr. Delmer's business.

PALEY. What! Who told you that?

RHODA. Margaret.

PALEY. And who told *her?*

RHODA. Her father.

PALEY. Her father's—mistaken.

RHODA. I thought you'd say that. Of course he is.

PALEY. Why! Do *you*, does *she* believe it?

RHODA. No, no; I knew there must be some mistake.

PALEY. There's going to be a battle between Margaret and Dr. West, but he could never descend to anything like that.

RHODA. Oh! how glad I am to hear you speak of him so! I wanted to be assured that he was not unworthy of Margaret.

PALEY. But why do you—?

RHODA. Because I want to save this family from ruin, and I want you to help me.

PALEY. I will.

RHODA. I must deliver to Dr. West and Dr. Van Arnem a certain packet, which will show them that they are the real owners of all Mr. Delmer's property.

PALEY.   What!

RHODA.   I can't explain now.   You'll soon know everything.   But the only way to save the Delmers is to reconcile Esther and her husband and bring Dr. West into the family.

PALEY.   He's ready enough to come, if Margaret will accept him.

RHODA.   You really believe he loves her?

PALEY.   Well, if I know what love is?   And within a few days I've begun to think I do.

RHODA.   Then he will love her just the same, if *he* is rich and *she* is poor?

PALEY.   All the more.

RHODA.   Now, I think that Margaret, in the bottom of her heart, loves *him*, though she doesn't know it.   But she would never marry him, in the world, if she were poor.   I want you to help me make a match.

PALEY.   (*Meaningly.*)   With pleasure.

RHODA.   Between Margaret and Dr. West.—You promise?

PALEY.   Solemnly.

RHODA.   Give me your hand.

PALEY.   (*Giving hand*)   With my whole heart.   (*He retains her hand a moment, and looks steadily in her face.   She drops her eyes, and he releases her hand.*)

Enter ESTHER L. 1 E., *an open letter in her hand.*

ESTHER.   I don't know how this is going to end.

RHODA.   What?

ESTHER.   After staying away a whole week, to send a letter like this!

RHODA.   What does he say?

ESTHER.   That I must emancipate myself from mamma. Think of using such a big word as that to his loving little wife. Now, I'm going to be just as bad to him.   I'm wearing a dress he can't bear.   You told him about the ball, Paley?

PALEY.   Yes.

ESTHER.   And that I expected to have a glorious time? (*Voice breaking.*)

PALEY.   I did.   (*Aside.*)   Oh! let us be joyful!—but we can't

ESTHER.   He will find that I don't care, if he *is* away from me.   I'm not going to miss a dance to-night.

RHODA.   But you wrote him you were ill.

ESTHER.   And he says, in his letter, I shall have medical advice at once.   (*Sleigh-bells heard, at first distant, afterward distinct.*

PALEY.   Yes, and he enjoined upon me that, at half-past nine, you should be here in the conservatory.

ESTHER.   Then he's coming.

RHODA.   But it's half-past nine now.

PALEY.   And there's the sleigh.

ESTHER.   Sure enough.

PALEY.   (*At door* R.)   Shall I say you are here?

ESTHER. (*Urging him off.*) Yes, yes, Paley, go! quick! quick!
(*Exit Paley* R. ESTHER *claps her hands and laughs.*) Rhoda,
he's come! he's actually come! (*Mock seriousness.*) In this
letter, he insists on *my* going to *him.*

RHODA. And you would not?

ESTHER. N—n—no! The woman who shows herself only once
submissive to her husband, is lost. Mamma said so. Mamma
can prove it by the most astounding examples. I'm going to
show him that I'm perfectly indifferent. I *am* indifferent.
(*Looking off* R.) How long he is!

RHODA. He's talking to Paley. (*She has been looking out
anxiously.*)

ESTHER. When he sees this dress, he'll see that *I* don't intend to yield.

RHODA. You'd better meet him half way.

ESTHER. When *he* has already come the *whole* way. You
silly girl!

RHODA. (*Turning to her.*) But Esther—

ESTHER. I tell you, I shall see him here—yes, at my feet.

RHODA. Some one's coming up the walk.

ESTHER. (*With a half-suppressed cry of joy.*) It's he! Dear
Fred! How I tremble! (*She seizes* RHODA'S *hand. They both
stand* C., *listening intently, but not looking.*) I hear his footsteps. A moment more! Oh! it seems a week. (*Keeping
time with her head as she speaks.*) Nearer—nearer—nearer!
(*Door* R. *opens.*) Here he is! Fred!! (*She turns with a cry of
joy.*)

Enter WEST R., *quickly closing the door after him.*

WEST. Good-evening, Mrs. Van Arnem.

ESTHER. (*Starting back.*) Good heavens! not Fred! (*At
first sight of* WEST, RHODA *has withdrawn up* L., *with exclamation
of fear, and stands regarding him intently.*)

WEST. Fred? Were you expecting Fred?—Miss Manly.
(*Bows.*)

RHODA. (*Bowing and in faint voice.*) Dr. West. (*Enter
PALEY* R., *and speaks aside with* WEST. *As soon as* WEST *turns
from* RHODA, *she catches the door-post* L. 3 E. *to steady herself;
then, aside.*) I must get—the packet. (*With quick look at*
WEST, *exit* L. 3 E.)

WEST. (*Apart to* PALEY.) I think, on the whole, Mr. and
Mrs. Delmer too, had better know of my presence here. (*Exit
PALEY* L. 1 E. WEST *crosses and looks after him. Aside.*)
I'm the last guest in the world they expected to-night. Now,
fair cousin—

ESTHER. Outrageous!

WEST. What?

ESTHER. *Your* coming.

WEST. You sent word that you were ill.

ESTHER. And Fred—Dr. Van Arnem said *he'd* come.

WEST. Pardon me. He promised medical advice, and I am
at your service.

ESTHER. You ?

WEST. Yes, hearing of this ball, and that you, though ill,
were hurling yourself into the mad vortex of pleasure, we grew
alarmed ; so, in the immortal words of the still more immortal
Cassius, I said to my cousin, " I am a doctor, I, older in prac-
tice, abler than yourself"—(*Aside*) to make conditions.

ESTHER. Horrid man ! You tell him I'm well, and that I'm
wearing my flame-colored dress with yellow trimmings.

WEST. I warn you. He's very much annoyed.

ESTHER. He ! Better and better ! he worries and torments
his poor little wife, and *he's* very much annoyed. The world's
upside down. Here have I been waiting and longing—I should
like to know how *he* has passed the time.

WEST. Pleasantly enough.

ESTHER. Indeed !

WEST. After leaving here a week ago, he first settled everything about the little house at Irvington.

ESTHER. Yes.

WEST. Then we took the train for the city.

ESTHER. Well ?

WEST. After a pleasant evening at the theatre, having no
home to go to, we went to the Brunswick. The next few days
were spent in purchasing household gods—I mean goods.

ESTHER. Well ?

WEST. Last night, to celebrate the completion of a satisfac-
tory week's work, a little circle of us—old classmates—
supped at Delmonico's. Toasted everything we could think of—
good wives included—

ESTHER. (*With difficulty restraining her indignation.*) And
then—?

WEST. We took the—*morning* train for Fred's home.

ESTHER. His home ?

WEST. It would be, if his wife were there.

ESTHER. Does he expect her ?

WEST. Constantly. I think that letter tells you so.

ESTHER. It's a horrid letter ! There ! (*Tearing the letter in
pieces and throwing the pieces in* WEST'S *hat.*) Fred knows I'm
fond of him, and counts upon it, to bring me to him. Very
good ! I won't be fond of him any more. I'll give him twenty-
four hours—no, that's a great deal too long—twelve hours—no,
two. In two hours he comes penitently back, or—

WEST. You'll go to him.

ESTHER. No! no! By no means ! Most certainly not ! I don't
know yet what I shall do, but it'll be something dreadful. Tell
him that. (*Changing tone and speaking half pleadingly.*)
Won't you ? *Won't* you tell him ? just what I say ? Tell him
with an anxious face—like this—as if you didn't know *what* I
was going to do.

Enter DELMER L. 1.E., *unfolding a newspaper.*

DELMER. (*Looking in first.*) Ah ! He is here. My child, will

you leave us a moment. (ESTHER *peevishly stamps her foot
at the interruption, and goes up, and as* DELMER *approaches*
WEST, *she goes out* L. 3 E.) You *are* here.

WEST. I am.

DELMER. I'm glad—no, not glad, but—

WEST. I'm here all the same. I understand, sir.

DELMER. (*Pointing to column of newspaper.*) What's the
meaning of this?

WEST. Of what?

DELMER. This article in yesterday's paper. (*Reads.*) " *Vancouver and Portland R. R.—small and insignificant branch—
no possibility of road ever being built—most worthless stock in the
market—for further particulars apply, &c.*" Signed L. W. Can
you deny that those are your initials?

WEST. Not while Leonard is spelt with an L, and West with
a W.

DELMER. Then you wrote it.

WEST. I did. It was my duty.

DELMER. Duty?

WEST. I'm just from that section of the country; represent
the road, of which this is supposed to be a branch. Our own
interest compelled me to show the facts.

DELMER. You know the road's been projected, the line sur-
veyed—

WEST. And yet the Vancouver and Portland will never exist
except in the books of a certain stock-speculator.

DELMER. The Vancouver and Portland, sir, is—

WEST. In plain words, a swindle. *You* have some of the
stock, I suppose. No cause for alarm. I'm told that the origi-
nator of the scheme, whoever he may be, to hush the matter up
and save his name, has called in all the stock issued, and paid
for it dollar for dollar.

DELMER. So I did, sir; so I did.

WEST. (*Alarmed.*) You? you don't mean to say you are
the man.

DELMER. You didn't know that?

WEST. No.

DELMER. (*Sneering.*) Oh! of course not.—And I've spent
forty thousand dollars on the cursed thing. I'll lose every
cent of it—all through you.

WEST. (*Serious.*) I'm very sorry, but I give you my word,
I was fighting you in the dark.

    Enter MRS. DELMER L. 1 E., *with a newspaper in her
    hand.*

MRS. D. I only waited to find this paper. (*Holding paper
before* WEST *and pointing to a portion.*) You are the author.

WEST. The fashion column! Madam, I have not the honor.

MRS. D. You deny it? (*Points.*) L. W.

WEST. My dear madam, I have not, in my humble name,
monopolized those letters.

MRS. D. Can it be any one else ?

WEST. Since I did not write it, I must confess the chances are strongly in favor of some one else.

MRS. D. You haven't seen it, John. (*Reads.*) "*The lady in three shades of yellow and red.*" Who can it be but me ?

DELMER. (*Taking the paper.*) Who can it be but my wife ?

MRS. D. And the conclusion is an outrage.

DELMER. Yes, sir, an outrage.

WEST. (*To* DELMER, *taking the paper.*) Have you seen it ?

DELMER. My wife says so, and when she says a thing—

WEST. (*Apart to him.*) It's useless for you to contradict, I understand. (*Reads.*) "*The lady, whose appearance at the Charity Ball we thus celebrate, frequently airs her fondness for yellow and red, in a turkey-red victoria picked out with straw-color, a crimson dress with trimmings of old-gold satin, pale pink bonnet, beneath which the—*(Hesitates, *looks up at* MRS. DELMER, *then reads in a lower tone)—saffron yellow face—*"

MRS. D. You needn't read it all.

WEST. Madam, this is severe. They cannot mean you.

MRS. D. They *do* mean me.

DELMER. They *do* mean my wife.

WEST. But I protest. *I* am guiltless. This paper is a fortnight old. A fortnight ago I was in the Far West. This malicious inventor of the saffron yel—

MRS. D. That'll do. John (*with a crushing look at* WEST), our *invited* guests will miss us. (*Exit* L. 1 E.)

DELMER. Dr. West, I take my leave. (*Exit* L. 1 E.)

WEST. (*At door* L. 1 E., *looking after him.*) In the words of the dyspeptic Dane. you cannot, sir, take from me anything that I will more willingly part withal (*Enter* ESTHER L. 3 E.), except your wife, except your wife, except—I'm forgetting my patient all this time. My dear cousin, this illness of yours—

ESTHER. I need a change of air.

WEST. You should go to Irvington.

ESTHER. Mamma has planned a trip for me to Canada.

WEST. Ah ! the only air which will bring back the color to *your* cheeks comes over the broad bosom of the Hudson, murmurs through the trees that surround a little home in Irvington, and a poor doctor, sitting alone in his study, by the cosy fireplace, hears it moaning in the chimney.

ESTHER. Do you think if I—no ! Mamma says, if I submit but a little, Fred will rule like an emperor.

WEST. He wants only the empire of your heart.

ESTHER. From which he's turned away of his own free will. No ! no ! ! for the last time, no ! ! ! Let him return to *me.*

WEST. He will not. Rather through long years—

ESTHER. (*Half frightened.*) What ? (*Almost a whisper.*)

WEST. With such firmness of character on both sides—

ESTHER. You really think he would—for years—

WEST.   It looks like it now. (*Aside.*) If she only knew
what I know.

ESTHER.   Doesn't he want to see me the least bit in the
world?

WEST.   Suppose you find out.

ESTHER.   How.

WEST.   A short drive to Irvington.

ESTHER.   Dr. West !

WEST.   The sleigh which brought me is waiting at the gate.
See? (*He points.* ESTHER *seems very much interested, and looks
eagerly where he directs her eyes.*) Oh ! what a rejoicing there
will be, when the door of the little house opens, and, instead of
that horrid Dr. West, a veiled lady slips in and glides quietly
to the study. The door opens ! the man by the fire looks up !
there's a cry ! a rush ! husband and wife are in each other's
arms, and the wind in the chimney stops moaning and whistles
for joy, because they are together.

ESTHER.   Oh, dear !

WEST.   You'll go to him ?

ESTHER.   (*Hesitatingly.*) Ye-e-s.

WEST.   Soon ?

ESTHER.   (*Decisively.*) Yes.

WEST.   Now ?

ESTHER.   At once.

WEST.   You will ! Good ! You've been dancing and
mustn't go out in the cold. We accept the will for the deed.
I'll bring him in. (*Going towards door* R.)

ESTHER.   Bring him in ?

WEST.   He's out there now.

ESTHER.   What ?

WEST.   In that sleigh.

ESTHER.   And you wouldn't tell me? Fred, the husband of
my heart ! He loves me still—his stupid, obstinate little wife !
(*Proudly.*) I knew he couldn't hold out. Quick ! quick ! Dear
Doctor, tell him anything you like. Bring him in, bring him
in. (WEST *starts to go, she urging him, when suddenly she stops,
then runs and seizes his arm.*) Oh ! no ! Stop ! I've got this
horrible dress on ! He despises it ! Oh, dear ! What shall I
do ?

WEST.   Go, change it.

ESTHER.   There isn't time.

WEST.   You must make time. I'm certain, I'm sure, every
fold of that dress proclaims eternal war between you. Run !
put on another—the one he likes best.

ESTHER.   My white one.

WEST.   Yes, the white one. Meet him with the olive-
branch—a white dove of peace. (*Leading her to* L. 3 E.)

ESTHER.   I'll fly ! (*Exit* L. 3 E.)

WEST.   Just what a well-regulated dove ought to do. Fly?
I feel like it myself. (*Coming* C.) Victoria !

(*Sings.*)   Though not a bird am I.
            Joy's carried me up so high,
            That a pair of wings are essential things
            To bring me from the sky.
                        Exit hastily R.

Enter L. 1 E. MARGARET, *followed by* PALEY.

MARG. But, Paley, I don't understand. (*Looking around.*)

PALEY. I'm sorry to take you from your guests, but I couldn't talk with so many around ; and I have something which I am anxious to tell you.

    MARGARET, *crossing* R. C., *stops and looks out* R. *intently, as though something attracted her attention.*

MARG. Paley ! (*She extends her left hand toward him, without moving her eyes from the object at which she is looking.* PALEY *crosses quickly to her.*) There's some one going down the walk toward the side gate. (*Points.*) Don't you see? A man ! He's going through the gate. Why ! there's a sleigh standing there !

PALEY. (*Nervously.*) I—is there? (*Looks intently, then speaks in a tone of affected surprise.*) Why ! so there is.

MARG. I *thought* I heard voices here. I fancied, too, I heard the glass door shut. (*Goes to door* R.*, and tries the knob ; the door opens.*) It's unlocked ! (*She looks in alarm at* PALEY.

PALEY. D—don't be alarmed ; *I* unlocked it.

MARG. You ? (*At first surprised, then as she looks at him a second and at the sleigh, a light dawns upon her. Shaking her head, aside.*) Aha ! (*She then turns her head slowly, and directs a steady, half-angry, searching gaze at* PALEY, *who lowers his eyes.*) Now I understand what called my parents and Esther here a few moments since.— Paley, a few minutes ago you brought a letter from Esther's husband. He writes that he will take her away. Is he not waiting out there now? (*She has approached* PALEY *during above.*)

PALEY. (*Nods.*) Emulating the worthy example of a certain noted lamb, "waiting patiently without till Esther doth appear." (MARGARET's *attention seems attracted again in the same direction. Then she looks at* PALEY. PALEY *nods his head.*) Yes, he's there, too.

MARG. He ? Who !

PALEY. The one you want to ask about, but won't.

MARG. You mean— ?

PALEY. Dr. West. (MARGARET *indignant.*) You misunderstand him entirely. He's not trying to injure your father.

MARG. He certainly is. How I wish he were not !

PALEY. Why, it wouldn't be possible for him to do it—grand, noble fellow that he is ! Why, he's the most generous-hearted of men. (*Enter* RHODA L. 3 E., *with a large envelope tied with red tape and sealed. She is quick and nervous in her movements, and checks herself at sight of* MARGARET.) I don't even believe there's any danger to you all, if he *does* get the packet—

MARG. Packet! danger!

PALEY. (*Aside, frightened.*) Great Cæsar!

RHODA. (*With frightened look at* PALEY, *then crossing to him, and speaking in breathless voice.*) Paley, you've not told Margaret.

PALEY. (*Nervously.*) I—I—I—

RHODA. (*Crossing eagerly to* MARGARET.) Margaret, what has he said to you?

MARG. Something about danger threatening us from Dr. West.

RHODA. (*With forced gayety.*) Is that all?

MARG. There *is* something.

RHODA. Oh! no! no! I was afraid he had unnecessarily alarmed you. Paley, how could you be so—

PALEY. Stupid. Say it. Somehow, everybody hits upon that word to describe me. Henceforth my model shall be that ravishing but silent bivalve—the oyster.

MARG. (*To* PALEY.) But you said danger—

PALEY. I'm an oyster! Hear my oyster—austere vow. As Mr. Iago says, "What you know you know; from this time forth *I* never will speak word" (*aside*) until Rhoda says I may.

MARG. Rhoda, explain.

RHODA. Why, Margaret, I—

MARG. What is the danger?

RHODA. (*Speaking with great effort to appear unconcerned.*) If you must know, it's a business matter between your father and Dr. West. Business men are always in danger from one another, when they speculate, you know; and when there are stocks and—and mines—railroad shares, and—and so forth, one often has information that another wants; and, if he had it, could make a great deal of money, but the other one uses it, and—the—other—one loses money; but soon he gets it back again, and the other one loses it—and—it's all business—*business;* don't you understand?

MARG. I understand that you are keeping something from me.

PALEY. (*Who has been watching* R.) They are coming.

RHODA *starts with slight exclamation, and clutches the packet more tightly with one hand, at the same time extending the other to* MARGARET.

RHODA. Margaret!

MARG. You mean what father told me—about that railroad.

PALEY. (*With sudden thought.*) The Vancouver and Portland.

MARG. That's the name. (RHODA *expresses relief in dumb show.*) Is it so serious then?

PALEY. Pretty serious. Railroad and mining stock is about

as bad to handle as dynamite. When they burst they go, and when they *do* go, you can't find enough of a man's worldly goods to hold an inquest over.

MARG. Dr. West would make my father poor? (*Broken voice.*) I would not have believed that of him. (*Shows some emotion.*)

RHODA. (*Apart to her.*) Margaret, you are in love with Dr. West.

MARG. Rhoda!

PALEY. They are here.

Footsteps heard outside as if treading on frozen crust of the snow. MARGARET *looks* R., RHODA *standing close beside her.*

RHODA. At least promise me not to be angry with him.

MARG. You see how much he thinks of me. He doesn't hesitate even to bring great loss upon my father. I'll never forgive him that—never.

RHODA. But, Margaret, dear—

MARGARET *is* C., *drawn to her full height and standing motionless, looking* R., *with defiance on her face.* RHODA *holding her left hand, stands partly behind her, though bending forward with her eyes fixed anxiously upon the door* R. PALEY *up* R. *Enter* FRED, *followed by* WEST.

FRED. (*Eagerly.*) Ah! Margaret! (*Looking around.*) Where's Esther?

MARG. Ask your cousin. Of late *he* seems to have taken control of the family.

FRED *turns inquiringly to* WEST.

WEST. (*Observing* MARGARET'S *manner, though at first about to reply naturally to* FRED, *changes his tone.*) I didn't like the dress she was wearing, and, as I have control of the family, I sent her to change it.

RHODA. She is so anxious to see you.

FRED. Not more than I am to see her. It has been hard to be severe with my dear little wife.

RHODA. (*Aside to* PALEY *down* L.) They are united again. That part of the work already done! and they shall help me do the rest.—Dr. Van Arnem, before your wife comes, may I speak with you?

FRED. Certainly, Miss Manly.

RHODA *goes up to door* L. 3 E., *as* PALEY *comes down hastily to* FRED.

PALEY. (*Apart.*) Do the square thing. Hush! She'll tell you everything.

RHODA. (*Holding door* L. 3 E. *open.*) In your study?

FRED. (*Aside*.) My *former* study. (*Aloud*.) If you wish. (*As he goes up*.) Leonard, will you—?

WEST. Certainly we'll excuse you. (*Glancing across at* MARGARET, *who stands* L.) I dare say we shall be sufficiently entertained without you.

PALEY. (*Aside, looking at* MARGARET.) Somebody'll be entertained when the storm on that angry brow bursts. (FRED *motions* RHODA *to go first. She goes. He follows. Still watching* MARGARET, *who is impatiently tapping her foot on the floor*.) The barometer is falling. The heavens are overcast.

WEST. (R.) Did you speak, Paley?

PALEY. Oh, I was remarking to myself that man (*glancing at* WEST *and* MARGARET) as a social animal was not always a success.

WEST. Tell Esther that her husband awaits her whenever she is ready.

PALEY. (*Crossing* L. 1 E. *stops. Aside*.) The last ray of sunlight withdraws from the scene. The storm's about to begin. And (*with sudden alarm*), great ginger! *I* caused it all. (*Looks at* WEST *and* MARGARET ; *quick exit*.)

WEST. Miss Delmer, I'm indebted to you for this opportunity of speaking to you.

MARG. Why are you here to-night?

WEST. Because I never give up what I've once undertaken. It's constitutional with me.

MARG. What have you undertaken?

WEST. To win the love of the only woman I've ever seen whom I longed to make my wife.

MARG. Your wife?

WEST. My wife. I came to-night—apparently for Fred ; really for myself—seeking for Esther—

MARG. Esther !

WEST. But also—for Margaret. (MARGARET *looks at him proudly*.) Don't be alarmed. I have prevailed with Esther. She will go with her husband to their own home to-night. I hope to be equally successful with her sister.

MARG. With me?

WEST. With you.

MARG. Your method of asking is strange.

WEST. I can't help it. I believe I never did anything like other people. If I'd been anybody else, I suppose I should have let the words you spoke at New Orleans shut you forever out of my thoughts. So far from that, I kept to my purpose, in letting you go from me as I did.

MARG. Your purpose?

WEST. Yes, and a week ago I came to let you know it. You were not ready to hear me, so I have waited until now. To-night I *must* make you understand me.

MARG. I will *try* to do so ; for this meeting must be our last.

WEST. It may be so ; it is possible that, at a distance, without our meeting, I can still watch over you.

MARG. Watch over me?

WEST. You have not forgotten the night when we sat together on the deck of the steamer, with darkness about us, and no sound except the throbbing of the engines and the churning of the waters beneath us, on our way down the Mississippi? Your hand lay in mine. The silence was broken. You said the life I had saved belonged to me to care for, to watch over—forever.

MARG. I—I know that I'm under obligation to you.

WEST. Obligation! I feared it. I was afraid you had mistaken gratitude for love, so I resolved to try you.

MARG. Try me?

WEST. I suffered you to misunderstand me; even, finally, to leave me in anger. Afterwards, three years ago, I sent you a letter declaring that I would call upon you this very month, but leaving you entirely free. I kept to every word, remained away until the time had come—all that I might know whether I had your gratitude merely—or—your love.

MARG. You are satisfied that it was only gratitude.

WEST. You are trying to make me think so. But I understand you better.

MARG. Indeed!

WEST. You are struggling to believe that you cannot be mine and I yours. But it must be. I cannot, indeed, conceal what I really think of your parents, but I am not unkind to them. I cannot woo as others woo, and you try to believe that I am cold—and unfeeling—and—insincere. Margaret, I can say no more—and no less—than I love you—be my wife.

MARG. You speak so to me, after what has happened?

WEST. Still more, for what has happened. Why! so far from loving you less; when I find you defending your parents, even against the man you love—

MARG. What! !

WEST. Then we'll say, against the man who loves you.—I love you all the more.

MARG. How can you say that word to me, after what you've done?

WEST. What have I done?

MARG. Shown me by your own acts, that you really look down upon me, as you confess you do upon my parents.

WEST. Oh! I have shown this.

MARG. During the past week.

WEST. And by my own acts?

MARG. Yes.

WEST. How?

MARG. Are you not trying to take my sister away from us?

WEST. To unite her to her husband.

MARG. Because you're ashamed of her family.

WEST. Because I don't wish to grow ashamed of my cousin. Come now, be-just.

MARG. I know, as well as you, that Esther belongs in her
husband's home. Under other circumstances I should be glad ;
but *you* are separating her from us, only—

WEST. Only for the sake of her happiness and that of her
husband, whom I love as my brother.

MARG. Your other acts cannot be thus explained. There's
no misunderstanding your conduct during the past week.

WEST. My conduct?

MARG. Even if I'd been in doubt, that would have decided
me. But I never doubted.

WEST. Doubted what?

MARG. That you would regard me, in some measure, as
you do my parents. I know you are unconscious of this feeling, but it is there—deep down in your heart—so deep you try
to persuade yourself that it does not exist, but, all the same, it
is there, and it stands an everlasting barrier between you and
me. You see, I can be as calm and speak as collectedly as
you ; because I want you to recognize the truth as I do—that
we must part—so that it may be in peace ; and then, for the
great service you once rendered me, I can retain forever a feeling of gratitude.

WEST. Oh ! no ! no gratitude.

MARG. Let us be reasonable, and say good-by—for the
happiness of both.

WEST. Would *you* be happier, then, if we parted for good ?
(*She turns ; he proceeds quickly.*) If I thought so, I would say
good-by to-night, and pass out of your life forever. For you—
why ! I would make any sacrifice. If necessary—yes, even
that.

MARG. Dr. West, I—I don't know what to think of you.
How you can say what you've just said, after such conduct—
Why ! your acts speak for themselves.

WEST. I've tried to explain.

MARG. About Esther and her husband. Yes. But your
efforts to injure my father.

WEST. Injure? I ?

MARG. I had it from him. Whatever else he may be,
he's honest, upright ; and I believe his word. He said he was
threatened with a heavy loss through you.

WEST. Through me?

MARG. I don't know the particulars. I didn't want to
know. Something to do with a railroad.

WEST. (*Starting. Aside.*) Ah !—Why, Margaret, do you
think that I—

MARG. I love my father—with all his faults, I love him.

WEST. You say you don't know the particulars of this railroad.

MARG. Will you tell me ? (*Looking into his face with an
expression of mistrust.*)

WEST. (*Returns her look. About to speak, then checks himself.*) No.

MARG. Then I shall believe—

WEST. I've done my duty only. I can say no more.

MARG. Dr. West, there is danger threatening my father at your hands. Paley almost told it, and Rhoda tried to conceal it from me. She asked to see your cousin alone. She is now showing him the proof of what I say. I don't know what it is. A packet, I believe. In the goodness of her heart, she's trying to ward this danger off, trying to save my father from you.

WEST. You are judging hastily.

MARG. Then you deny it?

WEST. I do.

Enter RHODA, L. 3 E.

MARG. When Rhoda and my father both say—

WEST. They are both mistaken.

MARG. Rhoda! Now we shall see.

WEST. We shall. Miss Manly, you are just in time. Miss Delmer misunderstands everything I do. From at least one accusation *you* can clear me.

RHODA. I, Dr. West?

WEST. She declares her father to be in peril through me; that there is some—(*turning to* MARGARET)—a packet, I believe you said—yes, a packet—the proof that what she charges me with is true. Will you be kind enough to give me information about this mysterious packet?

RHODA. (*Anxiously.*) Margaret!

MARG. Answer Dr. West Rhoda.

RHODA. Not here! not now!

WEST. Why, what's the meaning of this?

RHODA. (*To* MARGARET.) I told you it was a matter of business.

MARG. I want to know what it is.

Enter FRED, L. 3 E., *the packet in his hand.*

RHODA. (*To* WEST.) Your cousin will explain.

WEST. But this packet!

RHODA. He has it.

WEST. Fred, what in the world is the trouble here?

FRED. Oh! nothing, old man, only this came into my hands, and now it goes into yours. (*Giving him the packet. Then, as* WEST *is about to open it.*) You haven't time to examine it now; wait till we get home.

WEST. I'm told that this is the proof that I have tried to injure Mr. Delmer.

FRED. Who says so?

MARG. I, Dr. Van Arnem.

FRED. Well, Margaret, you are wrong.

MARG. You know the contents of the packet?

FRED. Yes.

MARG. Do they, in any way, place my father in Dr. West's power?

FRED.   What could have put such an idea into your head?

MARG.   Answer me.   I know that is what he's seeking for.

WEST.   Margaret, do you *want* to believe me guilty of what you say?

MARG.   It isn't what I *want* to believe, but what I *must*.

WEST.   I'll not hear you wrong *yourself* by speaking so of me.

MARG.   Then explain.   What are you all keeping from me?   What is that packet?   (*Pointing to packet in* WEST'S *hand.*)

WEST.   Nothing *I* need fear.

MARG.   Be careful.

WEST.   I'll prove it.   Miss Manly, have I ever seen this before?

RHODA.   No.

WEST.   Am I in any way acquainted with its contents?

RHODA.   I'm sure you're not.

WEST.   And whatever is here is the truth?

RHODA.   Yes.

WEST.   You are sure?

RHODA.   Yes, but—

WEST.   Oh! I'm not afraid.   *My* acts are open—as noonday.   Miss Delmer, I hope it is clear to you that I haven't the slightest idea what this contains.   (*Spoken to* MARGARET.) But as I'm assured it is the truth, examine it yourself first. *He offers it to her.*   RHODA *starts forward in terror.*   FRED *comes quickly between and catches his hand.*)

FRED.   Leonard!

Moment's pause.—Picture.

MARG.   (*Indicating* FRED *and* RHODA'S *anxiety to* WEST.) You see, Dr. West.   You have yet to learn what it is to fight with such weapons against me.   Take from us everything we possess, bring us to poverty, *want* even, you will never change me—still less after this.   Now we understand each other.— Good-night.   (*Exit* L. 1 E.   WEST *makes a move to follow, but is intercepted by* RHODA, *who, with clasped hands and an appealing look, stops him.*)

WEST.   Miss Manly!   Fred!   What's the matter?   What is this?   (*Packet.*)

FRED.   Proof that her father is a scoundrel.

RHODA.   Oh, Dr. West! be merciful!

WEST.   I?   Why—see here!   (*To* FRED)   Tell me plainly what's the meaning of it all?

FRED.   It means, Leonard, that John Delmer's wealth came from money which belonged to our uncle, Richard Varry.

WEST.   (*Amazed.*)   What!!

FRED.   Esther's coming!   (*Crossing to door* L. 3 E.)   Here, Leonard, go to the study and examine the packet while I speak to her.   (WEST, *crossing, is almost at door, when* RHODA *speaks.*)

RHODA. (*In hurried whisper.*) Dr. West, Margaret believes in her father. You don't know what suffering it would cause her if she were to learn this. Have pity on her and on me.

WEST. Miss Manly!

RHODA. Tell me what you will do.

WEST. Let me first read this, and then I'll know. (*Exit L. 3 E.* RHODA *gives a quick gasp and makes one step toward door, with arms extended pleadingly, when—*)

FRED. Sh—h—h! Esther!

Enter ESTHER L. 1 E., *in white dress, trying to fix a rose in her hair, which, from nervousness, she cannot do.*

ESTHER. Fred!

FRED. Esther! (*Embrace.*)

ESTHER. You wicked, dear husband! No, we won't say anything about the past; I'm not angry now. All the time I meant to forgive you.

Enter L. 1 E., MRS. DELMER, *followed by* DELMER.

MRS. D. (*Pointing to picture of* ESTHER *in* FRED'S *arms.*) Didn't I tell you? I knew he was around, the moment I saw that dress.

DELMER. You've come to reason, have you?

MRS. D. I'm glad you've come at last, Fred.

FRED. I've come to say that my home is ready for its mistress.

DELMER. How? *Your* home?

FRED. I take my wife to my own house to-night.

MRS. D. What!!

ESTHER. (*With a timid look at her mother.*) To-night? *Evidently awed by her mother, and speaking nervously.*) Fred, you're unkind to me. I am good to you, when I might be angry, and—now you're beginning all over again.

DELMER. Fred, what's the matter with you lately?

FRED. I'll be plain. My eyes have been opened to my true position in this house. It was unworthy of a man who respects himself and exacts respect from others.

MRS. D. What are you going to do?

FRED. Take my wife to myself. I must be sole master in whatever pertains to Esther and me.

MRS. D. You want to rob this artless, inexperienced child of my protection.

FRED. To give her mine.

MRS. D. Oh! yes! You (*To* FRED) are to rule. (*To* ESTHER.) And you to *serve.*

FRED. I am to honor, and she is to obey.

RHODA. (*Who has during above been anxiously watching door L. 3 E.*) (*Aside*) Will he *never* come?

FRED. Esther, will you come with me?

MRS. DELMER *is about to speak, when* RHODA *catches her arm and draws her aside.*

RHODA. Don't oppose him. Oh! I can keep it from you no longer. What I feared has come to pass.

MRS. D. What you feared?

RHODA. The heirs!

MRS. D. Richard Varry's?

RHODA. Sh–sh–sh!

MRS. D. Rhoda!

RHODA. These are the men! I've told him. (*Pointing to Fred.*) And now—(*She points into room* L. 3 E. *and speaks in dumb show.* MRS. DELMER *nearly calls out in her amazement, but* RHODA *checks her, and they converse,* RHODA *evidently telling of* WEST *in room* L. 3 E. MRS. DELMER *looking there and at* FRED, *as if trying to realize the truth. This action is unseen by the others, who continue the scene.*)

ESTHER. I—I'd go through fire and water, to Greenland or to China. I'd share a crust of bread with *you*, pet, and not murmur, if it were necessary. But this is only a whim.

FRED. A whim, Esther? The honor and independence of your husband?

ESTHER. The peace and comfort of your wife? Don't forget the blazing cheeks and kitchen apron. I—I wasn't brought up to that, and I—I *won't* do it, there! If I loved you less, I'd yield to your caprices. You shall see now, I can be as reasonable as I am loving.

DELMER. Perfectly right, my child. I didn't give my daughter to you to take away from here. What have you got to offer her, anyhow? You want her to give up a home, where she has everything she wants, for such a one as *you* could give her? In your poverty—

FRED. (*Indignantly.*) Mr. Delmer!

DELMER. Oh! you may be a very learned physician, but learning doesn't put bread in your mouth.

> MRS. DELMER *and* RHODA *have gradually been drawing back from door* L. 3 E., *as though shrinking from* WEST'S *approach.* RHODA *merely moving around from front of door to side partly down* L., MRS. DELMER *crossing behind her husband, who is* R. *By her looks she has shown alarm at his words, and, at his last speech, lays her hand on his arm.*

MRS. D. John!

DELMER. Of course I don't mean to force my good money on you. (*Enter* WEST L. 3 E. *Stands listening.*) But the time may come, when you'll be compelled to remember that you have a rich father-in-law. Don't forget that "He buys dearest who is forced to buy and waits till the last moment."

> ESTHER, *during above, moves down* L. *to* RHODA. MRS. DELMER *seizes her husband's arm and looks anxiously into his face.* ESTHER *looks to* RHODA *for explanation.* RHODA, *with absent manner, her eyes fixed anxiously upon* WEST, *pats* ESTHER'S *hand, which she holds in both her own.*

FRED. You say this to *me* when, with one word, I could—

WEST. (*Coming in front of him.*) Fred ! !

FRED. Why not speak ? Why not tell everything at once ?

WEST. (*In quiet tone.*) Because your wife is listening.

FRED. Esther ! (*Grasping* WEST'S *hand.*) I'm a fool !
(*Crosses to* ESTHER.) My little wife. (*Very tenderly.*)

ESTHER. (*Meeting him* L. C.) Fred ! Why ! what's the
meaning of all this? I don't—

FRED. There ! there ! No matter, my darling. You leave
us here with your father a moment. Go, join your sister.
(*He takes her to* L. 1 E., *she still expressing, by her actions and
looks, her desire to know the meaning of it all. He opens the
door. She goes out.*)

DELMER. (*To West*) How dare you, sir, remain in this house,
after what has happened ?

WEST. Before I answer that question, I must beg these
ladies to withdraw. (RHODA *moves anxiously to* FRED, *with a
slight cry of alarm.* FRED *reassures her.* MRS. DELMER *has
moved* C., *somewhat back, crossing behind* DELMER *and* WEST.
There is a marked change in WEST'S *manner toward the*
DELMERS. *He is considerate almost to gentleness.*)

DELMER. You needn't take the trouble to answer.

WEST. I prefer to do so.

DELMER. Whatever we have to say to each other must be
said in my office.

WEST. (*Quietly.*) What I have to say will be said here—
now. (*To* MRS. DELMER.) Madam, may I request you to leave
us to ourselves a few moments ? (*Crossing* L. 1 E. *and holding
door open.*)

MRS. D. Don't be hard on us. (WEST *starts, and looks at
her in amazement.*)

RHODA. She knows ! I had to tell her.

MRS. D. It's so sudden. I wouldn't care for myself, but—
my—two girls.

WEST. I beg of you. (*Indicating door.*)

RHODA. (*Aside to her.*) Mrs. Delmer, do as he asks you.
Everything will come right, I'm sure. (*Goes toward* L. 3 E.,
where FRED *has first led her.*)

MRS. D. (*Crossing to door* L. 1 E., *turns.*) If I'd only known
before, I wouldn't have treated you as I did. (WEST *makes an
appealing gesture for her to depart. She does so.* RHODA *at
the same time going out* L. 3 E.)

DELMER. (*Who has been watching in blank amazement.*)
Well, I'd like to know what all this is about.

WEST. It will not take one minute, sir, to tell you. In the
year eighteen-fifty-seven, the news came to a certain man in
New Orleans that his two sisters, from whom he had parted
years before in anger, had been left widows, each with a son ;
they had become poor, and, somewhere in the far North—
he didn't know where—were struggling hard for a living. To
atone for the past, he started in search of them, leaving all he

possessed in the world—$75,000—in the hands of his partner,
a certain New Orleans banker—Mr. John Delmer.

DELMER. Me?

WEST. The man was Richard Varry—my uncle.

DELMER. What!!

WEST. The sons of those two sisters stand before you, not
to ask what you've done with the money, for that we know.

DELMER. You—you—know?

WEST. But simply to ask a settlement.

DELMER. You—you—don't mean to—

WEST. The night before my uncle left, he gave this,
(*showing packet*) to a friend, and told him what to do in case he
never returned. That friend was Rhoda Manly's father.

DELMER. My clerk!

WEST. John Manly.

DELMER. And this? (*Pointing to packet.*)

WEST. (*Taking paper from it and showing it to* DELMER.)
Articles of partnership, signed by you both, and an inventory
of the property. Is that your signature?

DELMER. (*After looking at it, sinking in chair* R.)   Yes!
Yes!

WEST. Here is John Manly's story of your ruin, and how
you saved yourself with my uncle's money.

DELMER. I don't care to see it. This is so sudden I don't
know what to say. I admit I've done wrong. I admit all you
say. But don't let it be known. For the sake of my daughters,
spare me that. Only keep it from *them*. You don't know what
they are to me, and if they—oh! man, man, don't be hard on
me. Don't take away their love. It's not for myself I'm begging, but for them. Do whatever you please with me, but
spare my two daughters!

WEST. You misunderstand me. I'm here for a settlement,
not to make a threat. The legal rate of interest is six per cent.
We will accept four. That raises the amount, in twenty-five
years, to double the sum left in your hands—$150,000.

DELMER. (*Amazed.*) What! that all you want? you ask
only that?

WEST. I speak of the matter to-night, because, during the
past week, you've tried to injure Fred's prospects in the city,
and, misrepresenting me to your daughter, have placed yourself
between me and her love.

DELMER. But now I'll—

WEST. Do nothing whatever, to influence her in my behalf.
I mean to fight the battle for her love, alone, unaided.   All I
ask of you is, to cease your unjust opposition—nothing more.

DELMER. She needn't know the particulars. I can tell her
you've saved me from ruin.

WEST. It is to prevent *any* interference on your part, that I
name these conditions to you. Not a breath from you or your
wife for me. Is it understood?

DELMER. (*After one or two attempts to reply; in broken voice.*)

I ain't used to such treatment as this, and it—makes me feel—kinder—queer. I—I'll do whatever you ask.

Enter L. 1 E., MRS. DELMER *hastily.*

MRS. D. (*Anxiously.*) For Heaven's sake! Margaret's coming. (FRED *and* WEST R. DELMER *and* MRS. DELMER *go up* C.)

DELMER. No fear of them. Great Cæsar! what these two are made of, I don't know. One thing certain : I never saw their like before. And I can't understand it *now.*

MARGARET *enters* L. 1 E., *followed by* ESTHER.

MARG. (*Speaking as she enters.*) I'll see for myself, Esther. This child tells me there is some trouble between you two and my father.

MRS. D. Margaret!

Enter RHODA L. 3 E.

MARG. Oh, mother, I know what has happened. They are trying to make you and father comply with their wishes.

RHODA. (*Aside.*) Be careful what you say.

MARG. The time for *careful* speaking is passed ; *now* we must speak *plainly.* Dr. West, I ask for an explanation.

WEST. Margaret, it is out of my power to give one.

MARG. You have *nothing* to say ?

WEST. Yes, one thing. Trust me.

MARG. How can I ?

WEST. You *must.*

(MARGARET *turns from him angrily to* RHODA.)

FRED. Esther I know trusts me. You will come with your husband ?

MARG. (*Coming between and addressing* ESTHER.) Sister, you owe something to yourself, to us. To-night is no time for you to leave father and mother. Don't you see this is Dr. West's work ? Prove your husband's love ; and when you enter his house, go of your own free-will.

ESTHER. Yes, Fred, I'll see whether you really love me.

FRED. You doubt me ? Then, good-by.

ESTHER. Good—good—by.

FRED. (*Moving* R.) I shall go alone.

ESTHER. (*Turning in alarm.*) Really, oh ! no, no, no ! (*Rushing to him and throwing her arms about his neck.*)

FRED. You force me to it.

ESTHER. Margaret! Mamma! (*Crying.*) I force him ! when I'm doing all I can to keep him. I'll hold you fast, so Now get away, if you can.

Enter PALEY L. 3 E. *with small travelling-bag.*)

FRED. Paley ! I'm ready. My wife will not go with us to-night. She will come soon. (ESTHER *releases* FRED *with a cry and moves away from him.*)

Exit PALEY *door* R., *not seeing* RHODA, *who stands as if anxious to speak with him.*

FRED.   We will meet next in our home.   (*Exit quickly* R.)
ESTHER.   (*Rushing after him.*)   Fred! (MARGARET *stops her.*)
WEST.   Margaret, you will understand me some time.
MARG.   Dr. West, you will go with your cousin.

General movement.   MR. *and* MRS. DELMER *start down.*

WEST.   Miss Delmer!
MARG.   I cannot doubt the testimony of my own eyes.
WEST.   Your eyes deceive you.
MARG.   Then tell me what has happened here.   Any one. (*As she turns to them.*) Silent, of course.   I know (*to* WEST) what that means.   But if my parents forget what is due to our dignity and self-respect, I do not.   If they fear danger from you, whatever it is, I do not; if they are willing to grant any demand, however slight, *I* am not; if they will not make the answer your conduct now deserves, I will. (*Facing him and pointing* R.)
RHODA.   ⎫
DELMER. ⎬ Margaret!!!
MRS. D.   ⎭
WEST.   I admit you have some cause for suspicion.   You have also the word of the man who loves you, that you are doing him a wrong—nothing but his word, for he cannot explain. This is not to try you.   I would tell you everything, and *clear* myself, if it were not a duty to remain silent.   It *is* a duty, so you *must* believe in me.
MARG.   Believe!
WEST.   If hereafter, you do not understand me better, then we *will* part.
MARG.   We part now!

> As they stand motionless looking at each other, the others watch the scene in breathless anxiety.   After a moment's pause, WEST bows and goes out R. 2 E.   ESTHER throws herself on her mother's breast, her arm about her neck. MARGARET quickly passes her handkerchief over her eyes, looks steadily after WEST, then suddenly giving way, she throws herself into rustic chair, and bursts into tears.   DELMER, who has been watching WEST, turns quickly, at MARGARET's sobs, and regards her with a troubled look.   RHODA, throwing herself upon her knees beside her, throws her arms around her.

PICTURE.

CURTAIN.

ACT III.

Scene—*The little home at Irvington. Cosily furnished room beyond which, at back, another is seen. At back R. C. is large old-fashioned fireplace, with andirons, tongs, etc. Left of fireplace, large double doors open into room at back, which is furnished in very light color and more beautifully than front room. From left-hand side of double doors runs a line of windows, with old-fashioned small panes, the windows themselves, broad and high, making convex curve to L. 1 E. Through these windows is seen the outside of the wing in which the back room is supposed to be situated, together with a window which looks into back room to left of double doors. Through this single window the light shines upon the back wall of back room, so that it is seen through double doors. The space between the line of windows and the wing on flat is overhung by branches of trees upon which is snow, the country being seen through the trees and, if necessary, a view of Hudson River. The sun is supposed to be shining brightly, and, through the windows, pours into the two rooms in a flood of light. There are shades, not curtains, to line of windows; to double doors portières drawn close. L. 1 E., door leading out of doors; R. 2 E., door leading into house; R. C., table and chair; large arm-chair by fire. Table in back room, also small work-stand. At rise of curtain, PALEY discovered in arm-chair, asleep before fire, newspaper partly held in his hand and partly lying on floor. Slight knock heard. PALEY stirs a little. Second knock.*

PALEY. (*Mutters.*) Come in! (*Third knock a little louder. PALEY speaks a little louder.*) Come in! (*Louder knock.*) Come in!! (*Very loud knock. PALEY in disgust turns chair facing fire, and curls himself in it for a good sleep. Short pause. Door L. opens slowly, and RHODA cautiously appears. Seeing no one, as PALEY is hidden by back of chair, she enters, looks around, then beckons. ESTHER enters cautiously and shuts the door.*)

ESTHER. I'm so frightened.—Rhoda! (*Beckoning with her finger. RHODA goes to her and listens.*) Don't you think we'd better go back?

RHODA. When we're already in the enemy's camp? You wanted to have a peep at your husband's house.

ESTHER. I couldn't help it, after your glowing description.

RHODA. You shall see that I didn't exaggerate a bit. It's a perfect gem of a place.

ESTHER. Yes, I *must* look at it. But suppose we should meet *them*.

RHODA. Paley said that Dr. West and your husband were sure to be away to-day. They were going to New York on business, and wouldn't be back till night.

ESTHER. But they may change their minds.

RHODA. Is that one of their characteristics?

ESTHER. (*Sighing.*) No. (*Regretfully.*) I never saw two men keep their word as those two do. They're positively disheartening. But it would be dreadful, if they were to catch us here.

RHODA. Why? You are the mistress of the house—even if you do not choose to live here.

ESTHER. That's true. What is Fred's is mine; isn't it? And I've as much right here as he has; haven't I?

RHODA. Certainly.

ESTHER. Even if I did meet him, I needn't speak to him, you know. You could say, I came merely out of curiosity, just to see how he managed to live; couldn't you?

RHODA. (*Smiling at her.*) Yes, I could *say* that. (ESTHER *gives a satisfied toss of her head and goes up toward the fire, looking around wonderingly.*) (*Aside.*) Poor child! a whole fortnight since she has seen her husband. But if Paley has done his part, as I've done mine, *these* two, at any rate, will not be separated much longer. (*Aloud.*) Paley promised to be on the watch for us.

ESTHER. (*Observing* PALEY'S *foot showing around the arm of the easy-chair, looks at it a moment, then rushes in alarm to* RHODA, *calling in quick succession and in frightened whispers.*) Rhoda! Rhoda!! Rhoda!!!

RHODA. Esther!

ESTHER. See there. (*Pointing.*)

RHODA. What is it?

ESTHER. A man's boot! (RHODA *laughs, goes up and looks to see who it is. Shows surprise.* ESTHER, *watching her down* L., *whispers.*) Who is it?

RHODA. (*Whispers.*) Paley. (*She beckons* ESTHER, *who goes to her. Together they turn the chair around from the fire, so as to bring* PALEY *in full view of the audience. He is fast asleep.*) This is the way he watches for us. (PALEY *shivers, and pretends to be pulling up the covering over him.* RHODA *motions* ESTHER *to move back of chair. Then, in a loud voice, she calls in* PALEY'S *ear.*) Paley!!

PALEY. (*Starts, sits bolt upright, rubs eyes, and finally.*) Must have been dreaming. I thought it was early morning and the milkman yelled. 'Twas my turn this morning to get up for the milk and see to the fire, and I haven't yet recovered from the effects. (*Shakes himself.*) To-morrow morning is Dr. West's morning; day after to-morrow morning, Fred's morning; and the next morning again my morning. (*Shuddering with comic horror.*) By-r-r-r-r! (*Gets up, and, turning chair, comes face to face with* RHODA *and* ESTHER.) Angels and ministers of — !

RHODA. And *not* the milkman.

PALEY. Ladies, I beg pardon. You must have come in—

RHODA. We did.

PALEY. Without knocking.

ESTHER. Oh! yes, we knocked.

RHODA. No, dear ;—(*to* PALEY) we pounded.

PALEY. Well I *dreamt* I—I heard a knocking, but I thought it was the milkman. (*With frightened look, turns to* RHODA *quickly.*) Did you hear me *say* anything ?

RHODA. No.

PALEY. Quite sure ?

ESTHER. Not a word .

PALEY. (*Relieved.*) I'm *so* glad.

RHODA. Why ?

PALEY. Because I also dreamt (*angrily*) I *addressed* the milkman. You see he wakes us up every morning.

RHODA. Why do you let him do it ?

PALEY. Well, as yet, we haven't succeeded in getting a domestic, and as we're all heavy sleepers, we made an arrangement with him—give him a cent a quart extra—to yell, until one of us makes an appearance.

RHODA. Who generally appears first ?

PALEY. Oh, always the one whose turn it is to start things for the day, see to the fires, prepare breakfast, etc.

ESTHER. Does Fred have to do *that* ?

PALEY. Well, when it isn't my day, nor Dr. West's, in the early morning light we see a figure, very much like your husband, flitting about his household duties. (ESTHER *raises her hands in horror.*) To-day was my day—which accounts for the way you found me. Fred and Dr. West had gone to the city and I had performed the after-breakfast ceremonies, clearing away the table and (*shuddering*) washing the dishes, so I sought repose after my fatigue.

ESTHER. And does Fred get tired once every three days ?

PALEY. Yes, every third day *he* sinks into that arm-chair, exhausted, just as I did this morning.

ESTHER. Rhoda I think of poor Fred preparing his own breakfast !

PALEY. Not his only, madam, but ours as well. For the present, we've adopted the motto of the three guardsmen, "One for all, and all for one."

ESTHER. And what do you have for breakfast?

PALEY. There is, about our breakfasts, a monotony, which, to say the least, is—striking. We subsist principally upon—tea.

ESTHER. Tea ?

PALEY. One morning we did try an innovation in the shape o' coffee. But (*shaking his head sadly*)—it was not a success.

ESTHER. (*Glancing sorrowfully at her.*) Rhoda !

RHODA. See what it is, dear, for a house to be without its mistress.

ESTHER. And the other meals, Paley?

PALEY. Oh! in them, as in everything else, we take turns. Though after *my* first *dinner*, it was unanimously agreed, that, in the interest of all parties, *my* duties should extend no further than lunch.—But you didn't come to see *how* we live, but *where*. Behold the mansion!

ESTHER. It's small, but everything is *so* cosy.

PALEY. (*Apart to* RHODA.) Show her her own room now?

RHODA. Yes.

PALEY. Remember your promise.

RHODA. You've worked well, but all danger is not passed yet.

PALEY. And when it is?

RHODA. I'll keep my word. (*Indicating curtains over doorway in whisper.*) Now.

PALEY. (*Going up to curtains.*) Mrs. Van Arnem! You haven't seen the *prettiest* room in the house.

ESTHER. Haven't I?

PALEY. (*Throwing back curtains, standing aside, and pointing to inner room.*) It is here!

ESTHER. (*Going to door at back and looking into back room.*) Oh! what a pretty room! Look, Rhoda! look! (PALEY *and* RHODA *exchange significant glances.* ESTHER *slowly enters the room, looking around and finally leaning against the table, facing audience, so as to form a picture.*) This is beautiful. (*Spoken half to herself.*)

PALEY. Fred fitted it up himself.

ESTHER. A perfect little cage!

PALEY. Bird and all now.

RHODA. Paley says Fred never comes home that he doesn't bring some little ornament for that room.

ESTHER. (*Thoughtfully.*) Truly?

RHODA. Do you know why, Esther?

ESTHER. (*Extending her arms, as she looks lovingly around, her eyes raised and filled with a tender expression, her voice low and full of pathos*). Because it is mine. (*Slowly she clasps her hands. Her eyes fall upon the work-stand. She raises the cover gently.*) See! here is my work-basket with everything I could wish—needle-case, and silk—and there's my name. (*Looks at it fixedly, then reads.*) "Esther Van Arnem" —and—here's a glove—torn. Fred has left it for his little wife to mend—(*tears in her voice*)—and there has been no little wife to mend it. (*Still holding the glove in both hands, she looks up, and the sight of the room seems to overcome her. She then looks to* RHODA *and extends her hand.*) Rhoda! (*moving toward her*) Rhoda, I'm a very, very wicked girl. (*Throws one arm about* RHODA'S *neck and bursts into tears.*)

WEST. (*Outside.*) What ho! Paley!

PALEY. Great ginger! Dr. West is back again.

FRED. (*Outside.*) Paley! where are you?

PALEY. Dr. Van Arnem! what's brought them home, I wonder?

ESTHER. (*In alarm.*) What shall we do?

RHODA. Stay and receive them.

ESTHER. I shouldn't know what to say. Paley! can't we get out without their seeing us?

RHODA. Are you afraid to meet your husband?

ESTHER. (*After a glance at the back room, which seems to decide her, turning to* RHODA, *firmly*) No. But I must have time to think. (*Going down* L. *and turning to them.*) Oh! don't be alarmed. The mistress of such a dear little home won't be long away from it.

PALEY. Good!

ESTHER. Tell me how we can get out.

PALEY. The same way you came in. Go right down the walk. They can't see you.

ESTHER. Come, Rhoda! Paley! I want you to help me.

PALEY. I'll join you. Quick! or you'll be too late.

ESTHER. Dear Fred! you shan't wait long now for your little wife.

RHODA. They are here. (*Exeunt* RHODA *and* ESTHER L. 1 E.)

PALEY. (*Crossing to door* R. *and looking out.*) Fortunately they took the short cut and came up from the station by the back way.

Enter WEST *rapidly* R., *looking back.*

WEST. (*In hurried whisper.*) Well, did she come?

PALEY. Just gone out by the front way.

WEST. (*Crossing* L.) Gone?

PALEY. Coming back.

WEST. Then your plan succeeded?

PALEY. With the help of Miss Rhoda.

WEST. Good! not a bit too soon. (*Crossing to door* R.) Fred, where are you? Come in and announce the good news yourself. (*Enter* FRED *slowly* R., *with very dejected air.* WEST *takes his hand and lays a hand on his shoulder.*) There, there, old man, cheer up! Why! who would think, to look at you, that you had just won a triumph? Come now! tell Paley all about it.

FRED. (*As* PALEY *approaches eagerly, in sad, careless tone.*) Paley, I've been elected.

PALEY. (*Aside.*) On a burial committee.

FRED. What?

PALEY. Oh! I was remarking to myself that joy was not *very* violently depicted on your countenance.

FRED. There's no joy in success, when she is not here to share it with me. (*Sinking in chair before fire.*)

WEST. Courage! she *will* share it.

PALEY. (*Aside.*) Sooner than he thinks.—I can't stop longer now, as glad as I am. Certain household matters demand my instantaneous attention. (*Moving* L. ; *then nervously.*) Oh ! there have been two girls here ; and I told one of them she might come and take the housekeeping just as soon as she liked.

FRED.   *Any*-body is better than *no*-body.

PALEY.   Nobody is better than this girl. I'm not much of a reader of character, but I'm sure this is *the* girl for the place. Besides, she's married, and her husband, Fred—can take care of your horse. I thought it would be nice, having husband and wife both here—and—and— (*Seeing* WEST *laughing.*) Don't you think so, Dr. West?

WEST.   Couldn't have anything better.

PALEY.   I—I've been thinking out just such a plan for a week past. You see, I know the husband ; he lives here at Irvington. (FRED *has his back turned to* WEST *and* PALEY, *and sees none of their by-play, especially* WEST'S *attempts to entangle* PALEY *in his talk.*)

WEST.   Have you spoken to the husband about it ?

PALEY.   Yes.

WEST.   What did he say ?

PALEY.   Oh ! he'd *like* to have his wife come.

FRED.   Why didn't he bring her, then, before this?

PALEY.   (*Continually motioning* WEST *to keep silent.*) He couldn't. She was away, stopping with some relatives near here. She only came home this morning. Finding we had work for her here, she decided at once to come. She'll be here soon, with her husband.

FRED.   Then we'll see them both together.

PALEY.   Yes.

WEST.   You're a capital manager, Paley.

PALEY.   (*Moving* L.) I'm going to see about them now.

WEST.   Have you to go far, Paley ?

PALEY.   (*Nervously.*) N—not very. (*Moving again.*)

WEST.   You say he lives here at Irvington ?

PALEY.   (*Very nervous.*) Yes.

WEST.   Where ?

PALEY.   Why—er—he—er—Oh ! you mean where is their home ?

WEST.   Yes.

PALEY.   (*With sudden thought.*) Here ! I'll show you. (*Leading* WEST *to window.*) You can see from this window. See that house over yonder ? (*Points.*)

WEST.   Yes. (*Amused.*)

PALEY.   The next one to this.

WEST.   Yes.

PALEY.   (*Pointedly.*) Well, he lives in the very next one to that. (*Look of triumph at* WEST, *and quick exit* L.1 E.)

FRED.   Two weeks are gone by, and Esther is not here. Leonard, how long must I wait ?

WEST.   Until she comes.

FRED.   That may be—

WEST. No matter when. A week, a month, a year, if necessary.

FRED. I am causing her the first sorrow she ever felt in her life.

WEST. Then you are laying the foundation for the first happiness.

FRED. Happiness! Why, whenever she appeared, she scattered light and joy over everything.

WEST. Then let her appear here.

FRED. Flowers seemed to blossom under her feet, wherever she stepped.

WEST. (*Looking around floor.*) Then I prophesy, these rooms shall yet be flower gardens.

FRED. Leonard, she was never born to suffer. She was made to be carried over the thorns of life in the arms of love. And I have been trying to change this, to uproot a flower from Paradise, in order to plant it in a world of trouble and care.

WEST. And when the winds of experience in that world sweep over the little flower, it will nod its pretty head in thanks —yes, sir, thanks—that you took it from a *fool's Paradise* and placed it in a *woman's world*—a home.

FRED. What? she come here? I've no right to expect such a sacrifice.

WEST. Sacrifice? Making a happy home, a sacrifice? Our mothers and grandmothers thought it a privilege, as every *true* woman does now. And Esther's a true woman, only she hasn't been allowed to think. Sacrifice! There's no higher mission on the face of this earth than that intrusted to woman. *Man* is only a *bread*-winner; his very stock in trade is out of the earth; *woman* is the *home*-builder, the giver of happiness; *her* capital is from Heaven.

FRED. The whole world smiled when Esther was glad; and she was *always* glad—happy as a little child.

WEST. Sweet as that happiness was, there is a greater—the happiness of a woman, the true mistress of a true home.

FRED. But Esther's home is—

WEST. Here, in her husband's house, and nowhere else. My dear fellow, in this part of the world people are willing to live in hotels, in restaurants, in boarding-houses, anywhere, everywhere, except their own homes. I expect anything of society that allows such a method of existence. Look where you please for the source of most evils of to-day. *I* tell you, they are traceable to the want of homes. Give me a *home,* if it's a house with only one room and a chair. I say again, your wife belongs here.

FRED. No, it is not so. The change would be too great. I wrong her, every moment that I stay from her side. Dear, patient little Esther!—I give it up. I'm going to her. Leonard, I'll throw myself at her feet and beg her forgiveness.

WEST. (*Taking his hand and feeling his pulse.*) What a pity a man cannot feel his own pulse! Yours is galloping.

But (*looking around*) go on; free your mind; no one can hear.

FRED. I've tried your plan; now try mine; my heart—

WEST. Oh! let your heart alone. In a crisis like this, trust your head.

FRED. Don't try to persuade me; I'm going. Esther shall suffer no longer. (*Crossing.*)

WEST. (*Detaining him.*) She's not suffering; she hasn't had a chance.

FRED. I must, I will go after her.

WEST. Well, not yet; wait a little longer—say three days.

FRED. (*Starting.*) No.

WEST. (*Holding him.*) Two.

FRED. No.

WEST. Twenty-four hours.

FRED. No! No!

WEST. (*Releasing him. Then seating himself before fire.*) All right. Go ahead. Destroy your wife's happiness and your own. While you're away, I'll sit down here and design a coat-of-arms for you.

FRED. Coat—of—arms?

WEST. Yes, the setting sun crossed by a hayrick, surmounted by a thistle and one donkey—rampant.

FRED. Leonard! (*A knock heard off* L. 1 E.)

WEST. Now you *must* stay, to receive your visitors.

FRED. Who are they?

WEST. (*Balancing the poker.*) Go and see, my boy. (*Exit* FRED L. 1 E., *after an impatient gesture at* WEST. *Leaning with one elbow on arm of chair and looking* L.) If it's Esther she's just in time. Hercules's twelve labors were nothing to my one—of keeping this impulsive fellow here for two weeks. At times, I felt as if I could use Hercules's club to advantage. As a rule, where "hearts" lead, you'd better follow pretty closely with "clubs." (*Pause.*) Paley said there were *two* girls. (*Stops balancing poker, and holds it still in his hand. Slight pause.*) I wonder who the other one was.

Enter FRED L. 1 E., *followed by* MRS. *and* MR. DELMER.

FRED. (*Speaking as he enters.*) Yes, we returned early, that my cousin might keep his appointment.

WEST. (*Rising.*) And also that I might celebrate my cousin's election. Mrs. Delmer, good-morning. Mr. Delmer. Congratulate the successful candidate. He now holds, in our university, the position for which he has striven so hard, which has never before been held by so young a physician.

MRS. D. What! really elected?

WEST. Yes, madam, *really* elected.

MRS. D. John!

DELMER. My dear.

MRS. D. Is *this* what you said would happen?

DELMER. Not exactly,

MRS. D. What have you got to say now ?

DELMER. Whatever *you* say.

WEST. (*Aside.*) As usual.

MRS. D. Oh ! I always said Fred would make his mark.

DELMER. (*Apart to her.*) But you didn't say he'd make it across the Delmer coat-of-arms. There's no mistake about it, my dear ; *we* are wiped out.

MRS. D. Anyhow, Fred, I'm glad you've done well, and there's my hand—both of 'em. You know I *never* thought *ill* of you.

DELMER. (*Aside.*) She never thought of him at all. Fred (*crosses and gives his hand*), I'm glad too, but—I don't know how you did it. (*To* WEST.) He wouldn't even give the trustees a dinner.

MRS. D. Nor use a cent of what we offered him, and even refused to let his *father-in-law* spend money *judiciously*, just to make the thing sure.

DELMER. And yet he's elected. Either the world is going around the other way, or I'm asleep and dreaming.

WEST. No, Mr. Delmer, you are just awaking—awaking to the fact that there *are* men who think more of honor and honesty than of a bribe.

FRED. No matter now about my success. How is Esther ?

DELMER. It isn't our fault, Fred, that she's stayed away ; make him understand *that*, my dear.

MRS. D. I was perfectly willing for her to come, after the way you both behaved to us. (WEST *about to remonstrate.*) Oh ! but I *will* speak. You could, just as easy as not, have taken away our girls' respect, maybe love for their father, but you spared them and *him*, and that's a thing their mother can't forget. I know our girls are a long ways ahead of us, and—and I've made up my mind not to stand in their way.

DELMER. Now, my dear. (*To* WEST.) She would come to tell you, although I said the appointment was business.

MRS. D. There's no business half so important to *me* as the happiness of Margie and Esther.

DELMER. That's true. A day or two after you left, she says to me, "John, we are a drag upon those two girls." Says I to her, "My dear, we are an *anchor*." "If society," says she, "*won't* have us, it *won't*." "And it evidently won't," says I. "Then," says she, "let us stand down, out of the way, and give the girls a chance." Says I, "Agreed." And here we are—down.

MRS. D. Esther would have been here long ago, only Margie wouldn't let her come.

DELMER. But if Dr. West would just let me speak out— (WEST *shakes his head*)—just *one* word—the least little—

WEST. Your promise, Mr. Delmer.

MRS. D. But Margie's got some faint idea that—

DELMER. (*In frightened tones to* WEST.) N—n—not from me. I—I—I haven't opened my lips once, not even to—my dear, you *know*, when she's called him everything she could think of before me, that I never said a single word.

MRS. D.   She thinks it's still that railroad, and declares she'll sift the matter to the bottom. She rode over with us.

WEST.   Indeed. (*Aside.*) Then there's no time for *me* to lose.

DELMER.   I'm afraid she'll be here.

WEST.   I hope so.

DELMER.   What ! (*In alarm.*)

WEST.   Miss Manly tells me she can't go much longer without giving Margaret some answer to her searching questions.

MRS. D.   Well ?

DELMER.   What'll you do ?

WEST.   I made this appointment with you to-day, to tell you. Fred, will you and Mrs. Delmer kindly consent to examine carefully every room in the house but this one ?

MRS. D.   Yes, I *want* to see the home you've made for my daughter, and to tell you, Fred, how impossible it is for her to live without you.

FRED. (*Eagerly.*) Mrs. Delmer, I know the quietest corner in the house, and if you'll only give me hope that Esther's coming to her home, I promise to let you talk for the rest of the day.

Exeunt FRED *and* MRS. DELMER *through* ESTHER'S *room.*

WEST.   Mr. Delmer, our business will take only a moment. You brought the Vancouver and Portland certificates ?

DELMER.   I did, because you made a point of it, in your letter, but I don't understand.

WEST.   You will. (*He has taken a packet from a drawer. He opens the packet and takes out papers.*) First have the kindness to tell me whether this is correct. (*Handing a paper.*)

DELMER. (*Looking over it.*) "*Acknowledgment on the part of Leonard West and Fred Van Arnem—all claims of estate of Richard Varrya gainst John Delmer this day cancelled by payment of —*" (*Pause.*) It's for *you* to say whether it's right.

WEST. (*Who is looking over other papers.*) It is right.

DELMER.   But there's no need of this. (*Paper.*)

WEST.   A matter of business, Mr. Delmer. We are both business men.

DELMER.   Why, the wealth we've enjoyed all these years came from that money.

WEST.   We have claimed what satisfies us.

DELMER.   The law entitles you to everything I possess.

WEST.   Here is your receipt ; and here, John Manly's confession. It has caused his daughter much trouble and pain. You will, I'm sure, agree with me that we grant her the satisfaction of destroying this with her own hands.

DELMER.   By all means.

WEST *puts paper down on table* R. C., *in a conspicuous place for audience ; then hands the partnership paper to* DELMER.

WEST. This belongs to you.

DELMER. (*Handing checks.*) And these to *you.* Three checks amounting as you see to the sum which you are pleased to say discharges my indebtedness to the heirs of Richard Varry.

WEST. Correct.

DELMER. (*Holding* WEST'S *acknowledgment down and looking at it strangely.*) I never felt so mean at taking a receipt for money.

WEST. Now for the other matter. These, you say, are all the certificates of the Vancouver and Portland R.R. ? (*Laying hand upon papers.*)

DELMER. Yes.

WEST. How much have you lost by this unfortunate affair?

DELMER. Forty thousand dollars.

WEST. (*Opens check-book and writes as he speaks.*) Margaret, from questioning Esther and Miss Manly, as to what happened that night in the conservatory, knows I've done you some kind of a service.

DELMER. Yes.

WEST. She will not rest without an explanation. She believes I have made a sacrifice, to save you from loss, but thinks it is in reference to this railroad. She is coming to ask if that be true.

DELMER. (*Anxiously.*) Well?

WEST. (*Handing him the check he has been making out.*) I shall answer "Yes," and so prevent the belief ever entering her mind, that anything else has passed between us. That I may speak the truth, here is my check for forty thousand dollars. (DELMER *draws back in amazement.*) (*Firmly.*) I take no refusal. The entire stock of the Vancouver and Portland Railroad *I* buy.

DELMER. Well, but you—

WEST. Don't you see it must be done?

DELMER. But—such—a—price!

WEST. I pay it for the happiness of my future wife.

DELMER. Now, see here (*pointing to papers of R. R.*), this is only just so much waste paper.

WEST. Then let us treat it as such. (*Takes up papers and throws them into the fire. As they burn, he, still standing before fireplace, turns and, pointing to papers, says, in quiet voice.*) Is it clear to you, how the business of *my wife's* father must be conducted hereafter?

DELMER. I give you my word of—yes, of honor—I begin to feel what it means now—that you shall never regret your treatment of me. It has made me another man.

WEST. Then, to that other man I offer the hand and help of a friend. (*He extends his hand, and advances.* DELMER *seizes and holds it in a firm grasp. Second's pause.—Enter* ESTHER L. 1 E., *followed by* PALEY *and* RHODA, PALEY *carrying a basket,* ESTHER *and* RHODA *each a bundle.*)

ESTHER. (*Bustling about, taking off things, etc., her manner a little nervous. but yet calm.*) Ah ! we have visitors. Good-morning, Dr. West ; good-morning, papa. I'm glad you came over to see us. Did you leave mamma well ? I've been making a few purchases for dinner, and am too busy now to stop and talk.

DELMER. (*Who has been watching her in amazement.*) Esther here ?

ESTHER. Certainly, papa. Didn't you expect to find me in ? This is my day at home. Besides, to-day we celebrate Fred's election.

WEST. Your mother is here, too ; she and Fred are some-where about the house. We shall have quite a family party.

ESTHER. (*Who, at the mention of* FRED's *name, has dropped the rolls she was taking out of the basket, now speaks in a voice which she in vain tries to render calm, her manner growing more nervous to end of scene.*) And Margaret will be here presently. (WEST *in turn grows nervous.* ESTHER *crosses to him.*) You'll have to entertain her, for I've a great deal to do before dinner. Come, Rhoda, come, Paley, bring the things to the kitchen. (*Going up* C. *to room at back.*)

PALEY. You can't get to the kitchen that way.

ESTHER. Of course not ! What am I thinking of ! (*Goes toward* L. 1 E.)

PALEY. (*At door* R.) *This* is the door.

ESTHER. I declare ! It makes one quite confused having so many guests.

RHODA. We'd better prepare things here first.

ESTHER. Just as you say, Rhoda. (*To* WEST *and* MR. DELMER *who have been at the fireplace.*) You and papa go and keep Fred away till everything is ready, and (*to* WEST) come back yourself first, to see.

WEST. The mistress of the house must be obeyed. I will see that you are not disturbed.

ESTHER. Thank you, cousin Leonard. (*Exeunt* WEST *and* DELMER *at back and* L.) Now to set the table ! Rhoda, get my apron and cap ready.

PALEY. (*Opening cupboard door* R.) Here we are ! as fine a lot of table-linen as ever was bought.

ESTHER. (*Sitting down on the floor in front and pulling out linen in reckless and nervous haste.*) Here! tablecloth, nap-kins—take as many as we need. (*Counting.*) Five—six—sev-en—eight. (*Pitches the rest back.*) Put them in order, Paley.

RHODA. (*Having unwrapped parcel and taking out a dainty bib apron and a neat white cap.*) Now, Esther !

ESTHER. (*Going to her.*) Here we are! (RHODA *puts cap on her. She runs to glass,* RHODA *follows and puts apron on.* PALEY *spreads cloth.* ESTHER *fixing cap.*) So! little more off the forehead. Leave the strings untied ! All right. A pin. (RHODA *pins the apron to her dress across the breast,* ESTHER *holding the two ends.*) Well, how do I look ? like a respectable doctor's wife ?

RHODA. Charming !

PALEY. You look fit to prepare only ambrosia for the Olympic lunch.

ESTHER. Rhoda, you finish here, while Paley and I go to the kitchen. Take the basket, Paley, and go on ahead.

PALEY. (*Does so.*) To the regions of Pluto. Ganymede himself will show the way. (*Exit R.*)

ESTHER. Oh, how tired it makes me to keep house! (*Aside, as she stops at door R.*) But I'm at home. What a sound the word has! It goes right to the heart. Be quiet, be quiet, *my* heart; don't let any one see how you throb. (*Exit R.*)

RHODA. Almost everything is as I want it now. Margaret has no thought of what has really passed between her father and Dr. West. But she's coming to question him. What will he, what *can* he say? He's given his word, and that is enough. Yes. (*She moves slowly and thoughtfully toward table R. C., on which the paper left by* WEST *is lying. Stops. After moment's thought.*) There is no other way in which she could learn the truth—none. (*She has reached the table, and, at the last word, is leaning against it. One hand supporting her elbow, her chin resting on her other hand, her eyes bent in thought upon the floor, she does not see the paper. Holding the position a moment, then in a half-troubled tone.*) I wish it were all over, for her sake, as well as mine. (*Three distinct knocks off L. 1 E.*) At last! now neither of us will be long in suspense. (*Exit L. 1 E.*) (*A short pause when she re-enters, followed by* MARGARET.) Come in. There's no one here but me.

MARG. And I had made up my mind to meet *him*. I'm almost tempted now to go away again.

RHODA. Oh! you *must* see him.

MARG. Where is he?

RHODA. (*Pointing.*) In there, with your father and mother and Dr. Van Arnem.

MARG. I shall have to summon all my courage again.

RHODA. Why? What is there to fear?

MARG. You don't know what this costs me.

RHODA. It is only justice to him.

MARG. (*Looking anxiously around.*) Yes, that's true, but—

RHODA. (*Pretended alarm.*) You still care for him?

MARG. Rhoda! how can you say such a thing! Care for him indeed! (*Trying to speak calmly, but succeeding no better than* ESTHER, *though her manner is more quiet.*) The little regard I *may once* have felt for him has been destroyed by his cruel behavior.

RHODA. (*Smiling.*) You forget you are here now, only to acknowledge you were *mistaken*.

MARG. But there are so many other things to make me hate him.

RHODA. (*Appealingly.*) Yet you *don't* hate him.

MARG. (*Pulling at her glove.*) D—don't I?

RHODA. Not altogether. (*Tenderly, arm around her.*) Come, bend your pride; don't let it forever fight against your better self.　Now, tell *me*, your friend.　Don't you love him a little?　(MARGARET *has her back turned to* RHODA *and shakes her head.*)　Not the least bit in the world?

MARG.　Rhoda, why do you question me so?

RHODA.　Because I don't see how any woman can help loving such a man.

MARG.　(*Quickly.*)　Do *you* love him?

RHODA.　I *could* (*aside*), for what he's done for *her*.

MARG.　Then do.　(*Piqued.*)　You should have said long ago what was troubling you.　(*Trying to appear surprised and unconcerned.*)　It's nothing whatever to *me*, who loves him or—or whom he loves.　You'd never be happy with him, but—don't let any thought of *me* prevent your loving him.　He's nothing to *me*.

RHODA.　Nothing?

MARG.　(*With forced laugh.*)　Why, certainly not.

RHODA.　Then why are you afraid to meet him?

MARG.　He'll think I've yielded.　(*Quickly.*)　You know yourself, Rhoda, I came only because I didn't want him to suffer any longer on account of my anger.　Now, don't you?

RHODA.　You simply wish to acknowledge that you wronged him by your suspicions.

MARG.　I wish it were over and I away from this house.

RHODA.　Then we'll have it over.　I'll tell him at once you are here.　(*Going up* C.)

MARG.　Rhoda!　Rhoda!　(*Catching her by the arm.*)　Wait a moment.　(*Slight pause.*)　You are sure my motive in coming here will not be misunderstood?

RHODA.　Margaret.　(*Taking both hands and looking her straight in the eyes.*)　No one can mistake your feelings.

MARG.　It's all your fault.　You should have told me at once that the man had made a sacrifice for father.

RHODA.　But I could not explain.

MARG.　Will he?

RHODA.　He says so.　(*She starts a second time, but* MARGARET, *who has kept hold of her wrist, again draws her back.*)

MARG.　We ought to forgive our enemies; oughtn't we?

RHODA.　Yes, particularly those—

MARG.　Oh!　I make no exceptions.　It's my duty to act toward *him* as I would toward any one I felt *disposed* to forgive.

RHODA.　Certainly.　(*She starts a third time, and is held back.*)

MARG.　You are sure he will not think I am yielding?

RHODA.　Tell him so yourself; then any doubts he may have will disappear entirely.

MARG.　Then you'd better tell him, that I am ready to see him.　(RHODA *goes up back*; MARGARET *crosses toward* R.)　I will forgive him, if I can.　(*Crosses to table* R. C.)

RHODA.　(*Runs half down from* ESTHER's *room.*)　He's com-

ing. (MARGARET *seizes the table, as she leans against it.*) I'll leave you. Esther's waiting for me in the kitchen.

MARG. This will never do. I—I must appear calm. (WEST *is seen to cross the window of* ESTHER'S *room.*)

RHODA. (*Aside at door* R.) How I tremble. I'm as anxious as she is to know the end. (*With a quick glance in direction of* WEST'S *step, exit door* R.)

> *Enter* WEST *at same instant in* ESTHER'S *room.* MARGA-RET *has seated herself right of table, her arm resting directly across the paper.* WEST *starts at sight of her, and remains in recess.*

WEST. (*Aside.*) Too late! I left that paper on the table. If she chances to see what's written outside, it will be impossible to conceal the rest from her. Has she seen it? (*Coming down.*) Margaret!

MARG. Dr. West.

WEST. (*Noticing her arm over paper.—Aside.*) Why does she keep the paper under her arm?

MARG. You are doubtless surprised at seeing me.

WEST. (*Aside.*) If she even looks down, the words will catch her eye.

MARG. (*Aside.*) I *must* conceal my agitation from him. (*Aloud.*) Dr. West.

WEST. Margaret! (*Aside.*) To ask for the paper will only direct her attention to it.

MARG. I came that I might—

WEST. You are here. That is enough for me. (*He approaches the table; in her nervousness at his approach she clutches the paper nervously.*) (*Aside alarmed.*) Maybe she's seen it already.

MARG. I came only to set your mind at rest.

WEST. And what more could I ask? (*Trying to take the paper.*)

MARG. (*Rising, still holding paper.*) You misunderstand me. I came to acknowledge that I wronged you, and to apologize. Persistent questioning on my part at last compelled Rhoda to confess that you saved my father a great loss at some sacrifice to yourself.

WEST. (*Trying to get paper.*) She told you *that*, did she?

MARG. (*Drawing back.*) Yes, but not what the sacrifice was, nor why it was made.

WEST. (*Very nervous.*) Well, I tried to conceal it from you, but as circumstances have conspired against me, I must confess to a—*slight* sacrifice.

MARG. Father would have met with a heavy loss but for you; is it not so?

WEST. Yes. Of course you know what the loss was.

MARG. The Vancouver and Portland Railroad.

WEST. (*Aside.*) She has not noticed the paper. He would, without a doubt, have met with a heavy loss by the Vancouver and Portland.

MARG. And *you* saved him from it.

WEST. (*Glancing at paper, unseen by her.*) He isn't entirely safe yet.

MARG. Then your work is not complete?

WEST. No.

MARG. Do you intend to finish it?

WEST. If I can.

MARG. What hinders you?

WEST. His daughter.

MARG. Which one?

WEST. The elder. She holds in her own hands the happiness of us all.

MARG. (*In amazement.*) I?

WEST. You.

MARG. I understand. You have done enough to gain the father and mother, but not enough to move the daughter.

WEST. I would have kept everything from her, but by doubting the man she loved—

MARG. What! I love?

WEST. I beg your pardon; I'm constantly making that mistake; I should have said the man who loved *her*. However that may be, her doubts have forced him to admit what he would rather have kept from her.

MARG. Why keep it from her?

WEST. He hoped to be loved for himself alone. (*Aside.*) Oh! for that paper!

MARG. And he made this sacrifice—?

WEST. Because of his love.

MARG. Why, then, is it not complete?

WEST. I've told you. It depends upon you.

MARG. How?

WEST. By doing what I ask.

MARG. What?

WEST. Give me your—your trust. (*She is moving the paper nervously, holding it with both hands, and beginning to look at it, though unconsciously. He, observing this, redoubles his efforts.*) Look me in the face, and say you will atone for the past by believing in me. (*Again she is on the point of examining the paper, when he again takes her attention off by speaking quickly.*) I—I—I acknowledge I made a sacrifice for your sake. Don't humble me by making me confess the extent, for I—I couldn't do that.

MARG. Nor do I ask it. I merely wish to know how the completion of the sacrifice rests with me.

WEST. (*Very nervous.*) In this way. I made it for your sake. Now if you still withhold your *trust*—for that is what I need most of all—my sacrifice has been in vain.

MARG. I came to confess I had wronged you.

WEST. Yes.

MARG. And to ask your pardon.

WEST. Nothing more?

MARG. I don't see that you should expect anything more of me. I've forgiven you.

WEST. Forgiven *me*. Why. (*Aside, checking himself and changing his tone.*) Oh! to get that paper I'll admit anything. (*Aloud.*) Yes, Margaret, you have forgiven me, and have come yourself to tell me so.

MARG. (*Quickly.*) Not because I've yielded, though.

WEST. No—no—no, certainly not. *You* haven't yielded an atom. *I* yield. (*Extending his hands as he approaches her.*) Give me your hand—both hands—and I will tell you about this railroad.

MARG. (*Drawing back.*) No, Dr. West, I will leave something to my credit in the matter. I *will* not be altogether ungenerous. I came to acknowledge—and I say frankly—I have wronged you. I tried to make you believe I felt bitter toward you—when— (*Pause.*)

WEST. Well, Margaret, when—?

MARG. (*Quickly.*) When I did not. You have acted generously, and I refuse to be outdone in generosity. I confess that the whole trouble arose from my foolish pride. *Now* what have you to say? (*Air of triumph.*)

WEST. The only thing I've ever said, since we first met, "Margaret, I love you; be my wife."

MARG. I didn't come to discuss that. I think I'd better go. (*Crossing toward* L.)

WEST. (*Preventing her.*) Not until you've told me what I'd rather hear than all else you've said. Speak the one word, Margaret, that I've waited all this time to hear. (*Pause—she looks down. He draws nearer.*) Won't you?

MARG. If I were to speak it— (*He moves as if to take her hand. She draws back and continues quickly.*) I said *if* I were to speak it, you'd say it was only from gratitude.

WEST. I shouldn't want to hear it if I thought that. Can't you trust me?

MARG. (*Earnestly.*) Trust you? I—there, see what you've made me do. I've torn this paper.

WEST. (*Eagerly about to take it, to prevent her looking at it.*) N—n—n— matter about the paper.

MARG. But it may be something important. It was on the table there, and I never thought. How stupid of me! But it's your fault.

WEST. Yes, I ought not to have left it there.

MARG. Then it *is* important. I *have* done mischief.

WEST. Not at all. Why! (*Laughing.*) Tear it to pieces if you like.

MARG. You say that to make me feel easy. (*She is raising the paper to look at it. He catches her hand.*)

WEST. What! not trust me even in the matter of a simple piece of paper?

MARG. It isn't that I doubt your word, but—

WEST. What is it, then? (*As she laughingly raises her*

hand again, he again stops her.) I—I—I tell you what we'll do.
Suppose we make this the final test of our mutual confidence.

MARG.   A piece of paper?

WEST.   I—I know it's a trifle, all the better; it's a good test
case. I say that paper may be torn—yes, that I would like to
see it torn into a thousand pieces. You doubt my word. You
say you trust me. Well, I doubt *your* word. Now a very
simple act will prove that we may trust in each other im-
plicitly.

MARG.   What act?

WEST.   Tear that paper into bits. (*As she raises it.*) Ah!
don't look at it! (*Forced laugh.*) If you do *that* your confidence will not be proved. I haven't said whether it is important or not. I'll *not* say. Tear it on your simple faith in my
word, and I'll know you trust me. Tear it in obedience to my
wish, and I'll trust you forever.

MARG.   (*Wavering.*) It is so simple.

WEST.   Yet it is all I ask. Come now—the last proof you
shall ever give me. It shall be the answer to my question. (*Music.—She hesitates, holding the paper down in
front of her, and looking steadily at him. At last, her eyes still
upon him, she slowly tears it in two, then quickly into smaller
bits. WEST watches her excitedly, and as she finishes —*) You
do trust me?

MARG.   Yes.

WEST.   And love me?

MARG.   Yes.

WEST.   And you *will* be my wife. (*She looks up at him.
He catches her in his arms, then, as her head is on his breast, he
looks down into her face.*) At last! Now I'm repaid for everything. Oh! I confess it now—the doubt, the fearful anxiety,
the silence of these three long years.

> MARGARET *quietly places the bits of paper in his hand, still
> looking into his face. Enter* FRED *hastily at back, fol-
> lowed by* DELMER *and* MRS. DELMER.

FRED.   Margaret!!

WEST.   Ah! Fred, I said it would be a day of rejoicing. I,
too, have been chosen to a position of honor and trust.

MARG.   (*Giving her hand.*) Fred!

FRED.   I'm glad of this—but where's Esther?

MARG.   Esther?

FRED.   Didn't she come with you?

MARG.   No.

FRED.   (*To* DELMER.) You said she was here.

DELMER.   I repeat it. Esther is in this house.

Enter ESTHER *door* R.

ESTHER.   Quite right, papa.

FRED.   Esther!

> *She holds a large kitchen spoon in one hand, a plate under
> it with the other.* RHODA *follows, and* PALEY, *with a
> small dish.*

ESTHER. (*Quietly crossing to* FRED.) Have the kindness to taste this soup, Fred. How d' ye do, mamma?

FRED. Esther! what happiness!

ESTHER. Misfortune, you mean ; the soup is too salt. Taste it. Either Rhoda or I must be in love.

FRED. Dear little wife! To my heart!

ESTHER. (*Drawing back quickly.*) No, no, no! you'll spill the soup all over you.

FRED. Don't jest with me now.

ESTHER. I'm not jesting ; it's a very important matter, whether the soup is too salt or not. (*Holds out spoon to him.*) Here!

FRED. But, Esther—

ESTHER. Fred, you *must* first taste what I have cooked.

FRED. You? I will. (*Tastes, and makes a wry face.*)

ESTHER. There ! how do you like your little housewife.

FRED. She is beautiful.

ESTHER. And the soup ?

FRED. Excellent.

ESTHER. (*Aside.*) At least a handful of salt in it !—Really excellent.

FRED. Delicious.

ESTHER. (*Giving plate, spoon, etc., to* RHODA.) Take it away. I have undeniable proof that you are under my slipper, so come to my—kitchen apron.

FRED. (*Taking her in his arms.*) Under it beats the best and bravest heart in the world.

ESTHER. And you beg my forgiveness ?

FRED. Yes.

MRS. DELMER. *I* do, dear, for having kept you so long away from home.

DELMER. (*To* MARGARET.) And *I* for having kept you so long from *him.* (*Pointing to* WEST, *then embraces her.*)

PALEY *has taken dishes from* RHODA *and moved to table.*
MRS. DELMER *joins* MARGARET *and embraces her.*
WEST *has met* RHODA *by table* R. C.

RHODA. (*Aside to him.*) She is satisfied ?

WEST. Yes.

RHODA The truth is safe from her ?

WEST. Forever ! The only thing to reveal it was your father's confession.

RHODA. And that is— ?

WEST. Here. (*Placing in her hand.*) You are not angry because it's in such a condition ?

RHODA. (*Taking his hand and pressing it with a look of gratitude.*) Dr. West. (*Goes up to fireplace.*)

ESTHER. No, let the servants come to-morrow, Fred. To-day, the first day in our home, everything shall be done by my own hands.

FRED. Esther !

ESTHER.   You shall see what a perfect little housewife I am.

PALEY.   Don't you think that for to-day, at least, the dinner might be intrusted to me ?

WEST. }
FRED. }   (*Shouting emphatically.*)   No !!!

PALEY.   May I not help ?

ESTHER.   (*Extending her hand to him.*)   Yes, Paley.   (*To* FRED.)   Think what we owe to *him*.

PALEY.   Not half as much as you owe to *her*.   (*Pointing to* RHODA.)

DELMER.   (*Putting* MARGARET'S *hand into that of* WEST.)   Nor as much as '*you* owe to *him*.

MARG.   (*Looking at him earnestly.*)   I'll pay it all.

WEST   Your debt is more than paid in this.   (*Kissing her hand.*)   But, with Paley, I must admit, the secret of our happiness is there.   (*Pointing to* RHODA.)

> RHODA *is standing by the fire, her head resting against the mantelpiece, slowly throwing the pieces of paper in the fire.* PALEY *joins her, timidly touches her on the shoulder ; she turns ; he points to the two couples.*

MARG.   I don't think so.

WEST.   Indeed ?   Why not ?

MARG.   Because it is here, in— (*Hesitates.*)

WEST.   Well, what ?

MARG.   The power of woman's love.   (*Throwing her arms around his neck.*)

> DELMER *and* MRS. DELMER *are seated.*   FRED *is leading* ESTHER *into the room.*   RHODA *gives* PALEY *her hand, which he presses to his lips.*

PICTURE.

CURTAIN.

www.ingramcontent.com/pod-product-compliance
Lightning Source LLC
Chambersburg PA
CBHW021225260626
47172CB00002B/600